Cryptic Inheritance

Zane Clearwater Mysteries

Lynn Lipinski

Majestic Content Los Angeles

Dear Readers,

As I sit down to pen this letter, I can't help but reflect on the journey we've taken together through the pages of the Zane Clearwater Mysteries. It's been quite the adventure, hasn't it? From the very first case that thrust Zane into the tangled world of mysteries, secrets, and deception, to this moment, where our beloved protagonist stands at the precipice of a new phase in his life. I'm thrilled to introduce you to "Cryptic Inheritance," a tale that marks both an end and a beginning for our dear Zane Clearwater.

In "Cryptic Inheritance," Zane takes on a role that none of us could have predicted when we first met him. He's no longer the ordinary man caught in the whirlwind of extraordinary circumstances. Instead, he's embraced his calling as a private investigator under the guidance of the enigmatic and brilliant Loris Trapper. Their dynamic is one that promises to keep you on the edge of your seat, just as it did for me while writing.

But there's more to this story than just a career change. Zane's journey in this book takes a deeply personal turn. You'll have to read on to learn more!

Dear Readers,

As an author, it's a privilege to accompany Zane on his evolving journey. I've watched him grow, adapt, and overcome the odds with each new mystery he encounters. And I must say, I'm immensely proud of the man he's become. I hope you are too.

So, dear readers, fasten your seatbelts, for "Cryptic Inheritance" is a rollercoaster of emotions, revelations, and, of course, mysteries waiting to be unraveled. I trust that you'll enjoy this latest installment in the Zane Clearwater Mysteries as much as I enjoyed writing it.

Thank you for your unwavering support and for joining me on this thrilling ride. It's readers like you who make it all worthwhile.

Happy reading, and may the clues be ever in your favor.
Sincerely,
Lynn Lipinski

Also by Lynn Lipinski

God of the Internet

Zane Clearwater Mysteries

Bloodlines

Serpent Loop

Stalked By Revenge

Praise for Lynn Lipinski

Lipinski's natural gift for storytelling shines.

— Marci Bolden, author, *Life Without Water*

[Lynn Lipinski's] writing is magnetic, charged with intrigue, elegance, and grit.

— Marina Crouse, writer

If you have not read Lynn Lipinski, you are missing out! Well written, dark, and well thought out!

— Debra, Open Book Posts

This book is dedicated to all the people who told me they enjoyed reading about Zane Clearwater and his sister Lettie. Thank you for the encouragement.

Chapter 1
Zane

"You're the detective. You are going to have to crack the code of these stupid IKEA assembly instructions, Sherlock!"

Tiffany's voice dripped with exasperation as she dramatically flung the paper booklet onto the counter at her all-consuming Cell Phone Fixit store. The diagram stared back at them like the Cheshire Cat from *Alice's Adventures in Wonderland*, challenging the very fabric of logic.

Zane grabbed the instructions with a playful wink, hoping to earn a smile from his frustrated girlfriend. "Don't worry, Watson, we'll unravel this mystery yet."

He squinted at the diagram, then glanced at the wobbly disaster of a display cabinet. Dread settled in the pit of his stomach as the realization hit him like a ton of misplaced screws and wooden dowels—they had put the shelves on backward, and that's why the glass doors refused to cooperate.

He put on a bright face and tried to sound encouraging. "Honey, we've got a case of mistaken identity here. These cabinet sides are on backwards. No wonder the doors don't fit."

Tiffany put her face into her hands in disbelief before saying: "Oh great! We're never gonna get this finished!"

Zane chuckled, his fingers already deftly disassembling their lopsided creation. "Nah, just a rookie mistake. The clues were there the whole time. We'll have these shelves in line before you can say Swedish meatballs."

Tiffany grabbed an Allen wrench and pitched in with the deconstruction. Soon pieces were scattered all over the floor again like evidence in a crime scene.

"Next time we solve a puzzle, let's stick to crosswords," Tiffany quipped as they wrestled with stubborn screws.

An hour later, backs and fingers aching, they finally stood triumphant before a semblance of functional cabinets. The Cell Phone Fixit store would have to make do with their slightly wonky masterpiece.

Tiffany shot Zane a look that was equal parts grateful and relieved. "Congratulations, detective. You've cracked the case of the cursed cabinets."

Zane bowed with mock grandeur. "It's all in a day's work, my dear Watson. Now, let's celebrate our victory over the flat-packed fiend with a cool drink that doesn't require an Allen wrench."

It was about five o'clock when they arrived at her Midtown Tulsa apartment. Inside, she shouted out to Kayla Renee, her roommate, that she was home and Zane was with her. The next sound was the bathroom door closing.

Zane went to the kitchen to the left of the tidy living room, with its blue L-shaped sofa and about two hundred pillows of all shapes and sizes, for two cans of diet soda—the only kind the women kept in the house. By the time he returned to the sofa, Tiffany stood in front of the television, remote in hand, clicking through options on Netflix. She found *Mean Girls*, a movie she had seen at least a dozen times, and hit play. It was one of her adorable quirks: she liked the background noise and the comfort of the dialogue she practically knew by heart.

Zane handed her a soda and sat. "Ricky seemed scared to put more than a piece of paper in those cabinets. I don't think he thought much of our handiwork. Otherwise, he seems like a good guy."

"Thank goodness. Firing people sounds awful, so I'm probably stuck with my first employee for life."

"You're going to have to get used to that kind of thing if you're going to be a big boss lady."

"I still think of myself as an hourly employee. It's hard to imagine—"

"You own that joint." Zane clicked his soda against hers. "Here's to you."

A door opened and a woman's voice carried across the space. "Hello, hello, and goodbye."

Zane and Tiffany turned to see Kayla heading for the front door. She was a relative newcomer to Tiffany's world, and he'd only seen her three times. She was in her early twenties, clad in a black leather jacket, with a honey-hued face shaped like a heart and big brown eyes rimmed by long lashes that would have made Bambi jealous. From what Tiffany told him, she had just gotten her college degree in physical therapy at University of Tulsa and was looking for a full-time job in that field. Meanwhile, she was working the register at Boot Barn. Tiffany had told him her mother died last week of a sudden brain aneurysm, so he offered his condolences and noticed her eyes filling up. Before the tears could spill, she changed the topic to her planned trip to the grocery store the next day and left shortly thereafter.

Zane and Tiffany snuggled up for a bit, letting the movie play in the background while they paid absolutely no attention to it. Before things got too heated, Tiffany pulled away, reminding Zane that she was meeting her dad and stepmom for dinner, and he had promised his sister and grandmother he'd babysit his niece Milly tonight so they could go play bingo. He untangled himself with reluctance. She never had enough time for him these days. But no way was he going to make her feel guilty about it. She was following her dream.

In the parking lot, he was intercepted. He'd barely made it to the back bumper of his car when a woman's voice said his name and he turned, thinking he'd left something important at Tiffany's like his phone or his brain. But Kayla walked toward him with a tentative smile on her face. "Do you have a few minutes for me to ask you something?"

"Okay," Zane said. He glanced at the time on his phone—so at least he hadn't forgotten it. By his best guess, she'd been out here thirty minutes waiting for him. Something was up.

"It's personal," she said, smiling in a pretty but apologetic way, dimples emerging on her light amber skin.

"I'm sorry I brought up your mom and made you sad," Zane said. "It's just that I lost my mom too, a few years ago, and—"

"It's not that! It's not about you. It's about me."

"I've been told that before." His joke fell flat the moment he said it. Kayla was serious and earnest.

"Tiffany said you're a detective."

Zane raised his eyebrows. "Sort of. I mean, I'm working for a woman named Loris Trapper. She's a problem solver of sorts. Former police officer."

"Tiffany said you were in training to be a police officer too."

"It didn't quite work out." He glanced at the drawn blinds covering Tiffany's bedroom window, wishing she had warned him that Kayla was looking for help. But maybe she didn't know. After all, Kayla had ambushed him in the parking lot.

"But you still want to help people, right?"

"I do."

"Have you heard of cryptocurrency?"

There had been another big story about cryptocurrency all over the Internet just that day. For months it had been an almost daily occurrence, another person who turned fifty dollars into millions, all of it sounding like these tech geniuses had figured a way to conjure fortunes out of nothing. Then more recently, the spectacular fails: FTX with its polyamorous, puffed-hair boy genius and billions of dollars vanished under the Bahamian sun, the heaps of cryptocurrency touted by social media influencers, actors, and rappers that wound up being pump-and-dump con artist schemes.

"Yeah, I've heard of it."

"I'm looking for someone to help me figure out how to access a cryptocurrency wallet."

Zane laughed. "Maybe you need to hire a hacker," Zane said. Perhaps Lettie could help her. His faith in his sister's black box computer skills was strong even though he didn't have the slightest idea how she did what she did.

"I don't know a hacker I can trust. Look, I've never told anyone this. Not Tiffany. No one. But when Tiffany told me what you do—and about your family—I felt like I could trust you." The way she hesitated before saying the word "family" made it clear that Tiffany had spilled the tea on Zane's brutal past relationship with his father and half-brothers. "I'm not usually wrong about these things," she said.

"You don't need to blow smoke at me," Zane said. "So, what's the story behind the crypto wallet? You lost your password?"

"It was my mom's. I found it in her things, along with some evidence that Renee wasn't her real last name. Did you know it's the French word for reborn?"

"It's not an uncommon name."

"Not as a first name, no. But a last name? It's not that common."

"And it's not your father's last name?" His own mother had changed her last name too, from Davis to Clearwater, trying to protect him from his real father. The similarities were giving him the creeps.

"My father was a sperm donor. The way my mother told it, she wanted to have a child without the marriage or the man."

The creepy feeling stayed, but Zane's curiosity poked its head out. "When did she die?"

"Last week. Seems like yesterday and like ages ago, all at the same time. She died in her sleep at home. It was unexpected."

"What did the doctors say she died of?" Zane didn't want to let on that Tiffany had given him some of the details already.

"They said it was probably an aneurysm but we're waiting on autopsy results."

"What about your family? You have sisters or brothers, aunts, and uncles?"

"No. It was just me and Mom forever."

His life had been like that too, but he had Lettie at least. The parallels between Kayla Renee's childhood and his own were too similar to shake off. And he felt compelled to warn her off.

"Sometimes it is better to let things lie. I don't know how much Tiffany told you about my family, but you and I have some things in common. And trying to find out who my mother was after her death led me down some paths I wouldn't recommend. When people who love us, like our mothers, take a lot of steps to conceal their pasts, maybe we ought to trust them."

"Isn't knowing the truth better than not knowing?"

"I don't know if you want to hear my answer to that. It's not that clear cut."

"I'm all alone in this world. I thought you'd understand. I might have aunts and uncles, grandparents, and cousins out there somewhere. Why wouldn't I want to find them?"

Zane ran his fingers through his hair. "Because maybe they are bad people. Maybe that's why your mother built an entire life separate from them. Maybe she didn't want them to find out about you."

"I can pay you," she said. "Isn't this what you do for money? I have some money. I—"

"I work for Loris Trapper, so you'd be paying her. And I don't mean to be rude, but what you're asking is not that cheap to do. It can be a lot of hours of poking around and it may not come to anything. Could be two thousand dollars a week, minimum. I don't know if your paycheck from Boot Barn is going to cover that honestly."

She straightened her shoulders a bit and flashed her brown eyes at him with a little attitude. "I have some money my mom left me. Don't worry about that."

"What kind of job did your mom have?" It was a nosy question, but Loris had told him private investigators have to be comfortable pushing clients, or potential clients, for answers.

"She had some kind of IT job in real estate development. Worked at the same place as long as I can remember. We lived in a big house in Delaware Pointe for most of my life. I thought she owned it, but I found out after she died that it was a rental from the real estate company she worked for. That's where she was living. I've moved her stuff out of there already. Apparently, the rent is like twenty-two hundred dollars a month. Not that they were charging me that, but they sure wanted to make sure I knew it."

"That's a big rent check," Zane said. He still lived with his sister, Lettie, and her boyfriend in their grandmother's doublewide at the Majestic Mobile Home and RV Park in East

Tulsa. With his small salary from Loris, he was still months away from saving enough to rent his own place.

"Will you help me?"

"Let me call Loris, see if I can set up a time for you to come in and talk to us. But be sure that this is what you want to do. That you want to know the truth no matter what. It's not always what you want to hear."

"I want to know." Kayla Renee's eyes flashed again at him, and she put her hands on her hips for emphasis too. "I understand the risks."

Zane nodded. They swapped phone numbers and went their separate ways—Zane to his Toyota Corolla, and Kayla Renee to a new-looking Volkswagen Jetta.

He sat behind the wheel of the car, watching her drive away and thinking about her parting words about understanding the risks. There was no way she could fathom the risks at all. But he recognized her compulsion to find out anyway. The least he could do was try to help her and protect her at the same time.

Chapter 2
Zane

Monday mornings in the office with Loris Trapper started at eight o'clock sharp. She was a private investigator, licensed by the state of Oklahoma, operating out of a cramped office space given to her by Port Insurance Company as part of her compensation for investigating claims. The office sat on East Thirty-first Street just west of Yale Avenue, a commercial district filled with businesses in buildings that looked like homes with steep, chalet-style gable roofs and front doors with ornate stained-glass windows. The Port Insurance Company building was one of these, similar to the others but differentiated by tan bricks, dark shingles, and a square cupola on the roof that looked like a chimney. But there was no fireplace. Zane knew because he'd looked all around for one on his first day working in her employ.

Loris Trapper Investigations occupied a small, enclosed room at the back of a large open space filled with "hot" desks that any of the insurance agents could use when they came in instead of working from home. This morning, only one desk was occupied, by a man in a windbreaker and a ball cap, typing furiously into a laptop.

Loris's office was painted white with a brown-on-brown flat industrial carpet. Her desk was convertible and could be raised to bar height to work while standing or lowered to table height to sit at. Loris had the desk up high this morning, a good sign for a Monday morning because she usually chose to stand when she was caffeinated and excited about something. Maybe the prospect of Kayla Renee's job had intrigued her.

"Good morning, boss," he said, walking to the landline desk phone to see if the voicemail light was flashing. It wasn't. It never was, but checking it was part of his job.

"Don't call me that," she said. "Makes me feel old."

Zane shrugged. "You sign the paychecks."

"Speaking of that, I want to talk to you about the Kayla Renee business. I'd like to give you a finder's fee for bringing it in. Ten percent of the total, on top of your regular hourly rate."

Zane shouldered out of his jacket and laid it across the chair next to the filing cabinet. "I didn't expect that. That would be cool."

"It's only right," she said without turning from her computer. That's how Loris was, Zane had learned over the few months they had worked together. Professional and direct, not warm, and fuzzy. The kind of person who likes routines and rules in the office, probably because life and work outside these walls could be so unpredictable. In any given month, she juggled some fifteen to twenty cases, not all of them urgent.

The first hour of the morning was her paperwork time. Loris believed in getting the boring stuff out of the way first, so she forced herself to do the insurance company forms and reports first thing while Zane checked the voicemail, the general email box, and Twitter and Facebook direct messages to see if any new business leads popped up overnight. He had also been trying to build up the agency's profile online, putting together a basic website with one of those turnkey services for do-it-yourselfers. His tech skills were nothing like Lettie's, but he was proud of the modern-looking site he'd made for Loris Trapper Investigations. All this digital housekeeping always took longer than he expected, so when the knock on the office's open door came, he glanced at his phone to see it was already nine-thirty. Kayla Renee had arrived.

"Hello, is now a good time?"

Loris stopped typing and turned to face her, hand outstretched for a shake. Kayla Renee extended hers kind of limply, like Zane thought the Queen of England might do, and let Loris put in all the effort. They exchanged names and nice-to-meet-you's, all the while giving each other the once-over. Kayla Renee carried a huge brown tote bag with some designer initials all over it that stood out against her all-black ensemble of slim-fitting pants and a sweater. Zane didn't know much about women's clothing and purses, but Kayla Renee's sure looked like she didn't get them at the thrift store where he and Lettie shopped.

"Yes, yes, come in," Zane said. He cleared a stack of mail from one of the blue upholstered chairs and gestured for her to sit. Loris plopped into her fancy, webbed office chair, and swiveled to face Kayla while Zane shut the door and grabbed the third chair.

"I'm sorry for your loss, Kayla," Loris said. "Losing a parent is a terrible rite of passage and you're awfully young to have to go through that. But you didn't come to us for grief counseling. You've come to solve a problem. Zane tells me you've got a cryptocurrency wallet that you want to access, and your mother may have some other secrets."

Kayla's eyes, meeting Loris's, widened a little. "That's the top line, sure."

"Zane has already told you that sometimes hunting for the truth isn't worth it, right? In some ways, your story and his story are similar. A mother with a changed name, her death revealing secrets about how she lived her life. There is a chance it's not worth uncovering those secrets."

Kayla leaned forward. "It's worth it to me."

"And this cryptocurrency thing. It's like Bitcoin, right? Forgive my ignorance, but isn't that mainly used by criminals and scammers?" Loris said. "I get spammy emails all the time about buying digital currencies. Sounds too good to be true."

"It's a real thing. By that, I mean it has real value. I've been looking into it a lot lately. See, my mom left behind what's called a 'hard wallet' of cryptocurrency tokens. Last time I checked, that wallet has about one million dollars worth of crypto in there. But I don't have the PIN." Kayla frowned, not at them, but at the problem she faced.

Zane's voice rose high. "A million U.S. dollars?"

Loris's eyebrows shot up. "That's a lot of money."

"After my mom died, I went into her office to clear out her stuff. Her boss said they would do it and send it to me, but I wanted to do it myself. I wasn't too close with her and going through her work things, where she spent so much of her time... Well, it felt like it would bring me closer to her. Anyway, it was a lot of papers and mail and this small black gadget that looks kind of like a garage door opener or heart monitor or something. I asked her boss what it was, but he didn't know."

"What's his name?"

"His name is Terry Pickert. He owns the real estate development firm my mom worked for. In the same place I found the wallet, I also saw this sealed envelope that said, 'Property of Kayla Renee.'"

"You and your mom didn't happen to have the same name, did you?"

"No. Her name is—was Dawn. Anyway, I was glad I waited until I got home to read it."

"What did it say? Did you bring it with you?" Zane asked.

Kayla pulled a folded piece of paper out of her big tote bag and handed it to Zane. Loris rose from her chair and walked over to stand beside him.

It was a printed document with a paragraph of typed text, a QR code, and a handwritten signature. He read it out loud:

Dear Kayla,

This little device is a cryptocurrency hardware wallet. It holds the private keys to the public address of a virtual crypto wallet I set up for you. I know that sounds a little confusing. The bottom line is that through this hardware wallet, you have access to at least a few hundred thousand dollars, maybe more by the time you read this. You'll need a PIN to access the money should you want to spend it or turn it into dollars, and I've left that for you where you'll find it but not in this letter for security reasons.

With love, Mom

"See that QR code there at the bottom?" Kayla said.

The black box with its squiggly lines sat right underneath the signature line.

"Yup."

"If you scan that QR code with your phone, it takes you to the public address of the wallet where you can see how much is in it. That's how I know there's a million dollars in there."

Loris aimed her phone camera at the QR code and tapped on the link that popped up on her screen. She held her phone at arm's length so they could see the device. A white screen showed an "address" with a twenty-five-digit string of numbers and letters. Underneath that were three boxes. The blue box showed a balance of 47.6 bitcoin. An orange box next to it said the equivalent U.S. dollar amount: $952,308.95.

Zane looked at Loris. Now she was staring at the hardware

wallet, eyebrows raised. Most people would probably be wondering how exactly a person turns real money into Internet money and if it was a big problem to turn it back into real dollars, but Loris seemed preoccupied with the actual piece of technology itself. She turned it over and examined the tiny print on the back.

"Can you take this device into a car dealership and buy a Tesla or something?" Zane asked.

"I don't know," Kayla said. "I imagine you just have to find someone willing to take payment in this digital currency and you could buy anything."

"I'm sure the Internal Revenue Service might want its piece of this but that's not our problem anyway. You say that this Terry Pickert didn't know what it was?"

"Not that he told me. I don't think he thought this device was particularly valuable. Not like a million dollars valuable. Mom always told me he wasn't a tech guy. Was reluctant to use email even."

"Did you tell anyone else about this?"

"Not yet," she said, casting her eyes downward. "I didn't want to get in trouble with the IRS, like you said, or whoever, so I kept it to myself. Then when I heard about Zane, I thought I would come and ask for help."

"Have you found that PIN yet? The one your mother said she left for you somewhere?"

Kayla shook her head. "That's why I'm here."

"You said you moved your mom's things out of the house she was living in?" Loris said. "Where is that now?"

"At my apartment. It turned out that a lot of the furniture and all that were property of the real estate company. So it wasn't all that much stuff that I could call hers. A painting, some books, computer stuff, her clothes and shoes and purses, that kind of thing. It all fit in five boxes."

"We'll need to go see those boxes and their contents and get any other information you can think of. Can we do that this afternoon?"

"I don't have to work until four o'clock, so before then, yes. But Zane mentioned that this can be expensive, so I'm wondering, how much do you think it will cost?"

"We charge three hundred dollars a day. I can't know how many days it will take," Loris said. "Could be one day, could be twenty. And we typically take a retainer up front of at least five days."

Kayla gestured toward the hardware wallet sitting on Loris's desk. "I have money from my mother's retirement account I can use if we can't get at that Bitcoin. It will just take me a few days to transfer it out."

"We can keep this digital wallet for you as collateral," Loris said. "We have a safe."

Kayla nodded. "I'll be relieved not to have it in my possession. It makes me a bit nervous like I'm going to spill water on it and ruin it or something."

"Zane, will you write out a receipt for this crypto wallet? That she entrusted it to us for safekeeping?"

Zane nodded, slid into his chair, and grabbed the prehistoric carbon-copy receipt book Loris kept. If Kayla saw the irony of getting an old-school paper receipt for a digital wallet worth a million bucks, she didn't let on. She just tucked the handwritten receipt in her big designer tote bag, said thank you, and walked out the door with an earnest "see you later" like a woman glad to have a plan.

Chapter 3
Zane

As he knocked on the door of the apartment Kayla and Tiffany shared, Zane thought about how best to talk about the new client with Tiffany. So far, it seemed like Kayla didn't want her roommate to know that she was a crypto-millionaire. She seemed like a quiet person, used to keeping secrets—just like her mom, apparently.

Tiffany would be at the Cell-Phone-Fixit store until closing today and probably well beyond if the past was any indication. So, there was no risk of running into her for the next few hours. Good thing because they would need the time. Loris and Zane had to learn everything they could about Dawn Renee from five boxes of stuff. They might get lucky and find something fast, but more likely this was only the start of a long journey to unravel the life of a complex woman who left her daughter unanswered questions and a million dollars in untouchable digital currency.

Kayla answered the door, looking more like a teenager than a twenty-two-year-old woman with a million dollars in digital currency. She had changed out of the black ensemble she'd worn to the office and into fleece pajama bottoms printed with kittens and a gigantic blue sweatshirt. Her hair bobbled in a messy bun on top of her head.

"Do you mind if I skip looking through the boxes with you?" Kayla asked. "I just dread looking at some of that stuff. It brings back a flood of sad feelings, and I just can't do that right now."

"Just stay close in case we have questions," Loris said. Zane was surprised Loris let her off the hook so easily. The human brain doesn't retain everything accurately. People left out details as they processed events, leading to skewed memories. Seeing objects can often provide clarity, disturbingly so. Kayla would have to confront some unpleasant facts during this investigation. Zane was sure of it. Why baby her now?

"It's all in here," Kayla said, pointing to the bedroom opposite Tiffany's.

The five boxes took up a corner of Kayla's bedroom, which was tidy and furnished with a full-size bed, a small computer desk and chair, a dresser, and a bookshelf filled with physical therapy textbooks. A mirror hung on the wall above the dresser, and over the bed in a wooden frame was a painting of a woman's face and shoulders with a tree in the background. It was an original painting too, not a print, because Zane could see the brushstrokes in the tree branches and the woman's hair. The only piece of clutter in the room was Kayla's designer tote bag and coat, both lying in kind of a mess on the desk chair as if she'd thrown them there in a rush.

Zane took the top two boxes from the stack and set them out, one on the bed and the other on the floor. Loris perched on the end of the bed and started examining the contents in the box there, and Zane did the same on the floor. They continued that way until all five boxes were opened and gone through, but nothing seemed too likely to be of help with the hidden digital wallet PIN. Receipts, a few greeting cards, an invitation to a party that happened seven weeks ago, two boxes of business cards, and a couple of credit card statements and bank statements, but no diary or journal or handwritten letters or hard-copy photos. Their initial examination suggested these boxes contained that weird assortment of mail, paperwork, and personal items that often wound up together at the very end of a move. Sticky notes with phone numbers and a to-do list with items like "file taxes" and "get air-conditioner filter changed." A tax extension document had her signature on it. Zane handed it to Loris who compared the signature to the letter that came with the digital wallet.

"Handwriting looks the same," Loris said.

"You all didn't believe me that the note was from my mother?" Kayla said. She had returned, much to Zane's surprise, and was frowning and leaning against the doorframe, arms crossed over her chest.

"We have to check things out," Loris said. "You could have been mistaken."

"It's nothing personal," Zane added. He had already learned that people don't come to private detectives telling the whole truth and nothing but the truth. Kayla could have been lying. It wasn't unheard of. But he smiled at her and was reassured when she gave him a small smile back. Trust was an important part of the detective-client relationship, but it had to be earned on both sides.

"Do you know if there have been any more transactions into that digital wallet since your mother died? Either funds coming in or going out?" Loris asked.

"No, not that I can tell. Of course, I'm not an expert in all of this so maybe someone who understands Bitcoin better might see something I missed."

An hour later, they finally finished going through the boxes and sorting out the few items that might be helpful. Kayla was settled across from them at the kitchen table—Tiffany's kitchen table, which felt strange to Zane. His eyes flicked to the door often, as though Tiffany would return early from Cell Phone Fix-It and catch him here. He didn't know why he had such a guilty conscience. It was just business after all, which Tiff would see if she did walk in.

Loris started in on the personal questions, and Kayla took them like a champ, barely flinching as the private investigator probed around for details. One thing became crystal clear. Kayla didn't know much about her mother. Possibly even less than Zane and Lettie had known about their mother. What she did feel certain of was that her mother had been more dutiful than loving. Dawn took a serious approach to life, working hard to give her only daughter a good life but using fear as an incentive.

"There were times I felt like an invader in her life. Or worse, like I derailed her life. It wasn't like she said that directly. She never did. But there was a bitterness in her, like the world had let her down and she deserved better. It would come out, especially when I disappointed her." Kayla paused and slumped a little in her chair, then started picking at a loose thread in the cuff of her sweatshirt. "It doesn't feel right to speak about her like this though, now that she's gone."

Zane knew what she meant. His own relationship with his mother had been rough and tumble. But even years later, when he thought of her death, he felt this emptiness rise to the surface. *We may not all get the mothers we want*, he thought, *but we still miss the mothers we have.*

"Did Dawn have any close friends? A boyfriend?" Loris asked.

"A boyfriend? She was seeing a guy named Gabriel something. I never met him, but she talked about him. I think it was kind of casual. I don't know of anyone else. She was friendly with Terry Pickert and some of the other people at the office, but I wouldn't say she was close. And I was away at school for the last four years. I lived on campus. And I know the University of Tulsa is right nearby, but I didn't go home much. I don't think she minded at all."

"How long did she work for Terry Pickert?"

"As long as I can remember. I don't know what she did before that. Honestly, I don't even know what she did there, other than something to do with computers. She was a real computer geek and just about as cold and calculating as a computer herself."

It wasn't a very nice thing to say about your mother, but Zane kept his face neutral and his mind open. In the few weeks of police training he had before getting suspended, he learned the importance of accepting what people said at face value and reserving personal judgment. His old instructor, Cal Himmelman, had said that often as an investigator you had to get people to open up to you. You had to relate to them and if that meant hiding your judgment when they told you the awful things they said and did, then that's what you did. It helped that Zane's natural tendency was to keep his feelings to himself anyway.

"What do you mean by calculating? Do you mean to say she was careful or more like she was cunning? Like she was scheming?" Loris anchored her attention on Tiffany.

"I meant that she was cautious. Almost to the point of getting frozen sometimes. She hated leaving town, for example. We never went anywhere. Just last month, Mr. Pickert wanted her to help him set up a new sales office somewhere in Texas, and she just did not want to go. She was so mad at him insisting. You would have thought he was asking her to kill herself or something."

"Did she go on that particular trip?"

Kayla went to the refrigerator to grab a bottle of water and took a long drink. "Yes, she did. I think it was to Fort Worth. When she came back, she seemed upset that he had made her go."

"Was there any connection to Texas that you know of? Was that where you were born?"

"No, I was born in Tulsa. St. Francis Hospital. Except for a field trip to Oklahoma City in middle school, I've never left Tulsa if you can believe that."

"Did you always live at the house in Delaware Pointe?"

"No, not always. There was the apartment over on Yale. The Chalet something. I remember the vaulted ceilings. I think I was about three years old. We moved from there into the house in Delaware Pointe when I was about eight and were there until..." Kayla held her breath for a moment. "You probably want a photo of her, don't you? You'll need that, I guess, for your work?"

"Yes, I was going to ask," Loris said. "I didn't see any around."

"No, Mom was weird about photos. Said she didn't like the way she looked in them. I made her take one with me at my college graduation and she insisted that I not put it on social media. She was highly suspicious of all those kinds of things. Tried to forbid me from even having an account on Instagram when I was a kid, but of course, I went behind her back and did it anyway."

Kayla grabbed her phone from the kitchen counter and started scrolling. "Here's the photo. Shall I text it to you?"

The file hit Zane's phone with a ding and he opened it up. The photo was shot vertically, selfie-style, with Kayla's smiling face pressed against her mother's tight-lipped grimace. Only her head and shoulders appeared in the frame, but it was a clear enough image of an attractive, tanned woman in her mid-forties. There was some resemblance to Kayla, but the cheekbones were more pronounced and the nose a little wider.

"You don't still have your mother's phone, do you?" Zane asked.

"I do. It's in her purse. It has Face ID on it so I can't get into it, but you can try."

Zane didn't hold out much hope of accessing the phone but made a note to ask Lettie about possibilities. By half past three, Kayla's energy for the onslaught of personal questions remained high, but Zane and Loris were fading. They'd matched Dawn's signature on the note, so they knew that was confirmed, but other than getting the photo, the afternoon felt like a prelude instead of a conclusion. And no sign of the all-important PIN. It would have been amazing to have found the PIN on the phone in some encrypted password keeper, but if things were that easy, Kayla wouldn't be hiring detectives to help. Instead, they had credit card statements and a two-year-old to-do list. They left her to get ready for her shift at Boot Barn.

"Tomorrow should be more fruitful," Loris said. "These things take time."

Zane agreed that he would meet her at the office in the morning so they could go to Terry Pickert's together. Then he drove off for the Majestic Mobile Home and RV Park.

But his mind was still running circles around the details, so he called Lettie on his way home.

"What do you know about cryptocurrency?"

"More than you, I bet," she said.

Zane could hear his niece, Milly, gurgling and cooing in the background and felt a smile stretch his cheeks wide. Just hearing that baby's sweet noises turned him into a puddle. It was ridiculous.

"Yeah, I get it, you're the computer science genius. No need to rub it in, little sis."

"You surprised me, that's all. Why does my brother suddenly want to know about cryptocurrency? Have you come to see how money and banking systems keep us poor people down? How digital currency makes a world where dollars and banks aren't needed?"

"Spare me the idealistic hype, Lettie. This is a real-world problem."

She laughed. "What makes you think those problems aren't real?"

Zane ignored her tease and gave her the details of the locked iPhone, the crypto wallet, and its missing PIN, leaving out the fact that the owner happened to be Tiffany's new roommate.

"Not sure how you're going to get into that phone without the passcode. And the cryptocurrency wallet is another tough problem, but people have solved it. There's a guy on YouTube who made a whole video series about hiring hackers to break into his digital wallet. These wallets provide a lot of security. I mean the whole idea is that the technology is so strong you can rely on it instead of banks."

"Is crypto hard to buy?"

"Not really. Not anymore. There's different apps and platforms that make it easy now. The hard part is separating the scammy ones from the good ones. But it wasn't always easy to buy. You used to have to earn it by helping mine it or by being given some by someone who mined it." Milly's cries drowned out the final words of her jumbled explanation of cryptocurrency. He would have to get her to go over it again with him to make sure he understood.

"I've got to go," Lettie said. "Cryptocurrency 101 is over for now."

Zane tapped his fingers on the steering wheel as he turned into the Majestic, his mind still traveling a mile a minute, such that he missed the first big pothole on the road. The Corolla kerchunked in and out of the microwave-sized hole with such force that he hit his head on the car's ceiling. One day, he thought, he was going to afford to live in a place without potholes.

Chapter 4
Lettie

Lettie knew she was an unusual sixteen-year-old high school student because she was mother to the most amazing baby girl, Amaryllis Lily or Milly as they'd nicknamed her, born just four months ago. She sat next to her boyfriend Angel on the bed in the mobile home she shared with him, her grandmother, and her brother Zane, propped up on pillows and pretending to do her history homework. But she was obsessed instead with watching Angel cuddling little Milly in his arms as if the baby had been custom-made to fit there. Milly's eyes darted from Angel to her, her fist waving in the air briefly as Angel bopped her on the nose with a smile.

Lettie paused to gaze at their reflection in the round mirror set between banks of drawers on the wood-veneer dresser. Soft spring light from the two wide windows cast the three of them in a soft glow. She had to smile at her own reflection. Her hooded snuggie-type of blanket made her look like a lumpy baked potato. Oh well.

Content, Lettie opened a new browser window to look through a cryptocurrency channel on Reddit. Her deep nerdiness also made her an unusual sixteen-year-old. She had always been smart, with an unusual talent for numbers. She memorized formulas easily in her advanced math classes, getting high marks without putting too much effort into tests or homework. Computer programming languages came easily to her. When her mom was still alive, Lettie had shared her interests in tarot cards and the occult, but for the past two years, the mysteries of computer networks were all she wanted to unravel.

She remembered the term "Bitcoin" popping up in her searches years ago and being intrigued by the idea. Her ill-fated gig with the credit card fraud ring that got her and Angel in a ton of trouble last year had taught her about cryptocurrency as the lawless territory of black market selling and hardcore libertarians obsessed with escaping government oversight. But cryptocurrency had also become something like a stock market where people put money into one of two hundred different digital currencies and made astonishing amounts of money betting the value would keep rising. Now it was practically mainstream as an investment vehicle, but not so much as a currency. Hadn't Matt Damon done a commercial for some online crypto marketplace during the Super Bowl once? Even so, the gold rush feeling had started collapsing this year with the epic failure of a trading platform called FTX.

Crypto crash or not, Bitcoin was still worth some money, and depending on when someone bought it, they could have made a million dollars out of virtually nothing. Back in 2010, for example, it was basically worthless. She did a quick search: the Bitcoin unit price today was sitting at sixteen thousand dollars. Sure, that was down from its peak of twenty-one thousand but still was nothing to sneeze at, as Lettie's grandmother Verda would say.

No wonder Zane's client was desperate to get into the crypto wallet. As some of the key players in the crypto space were being revealed to scammers, con artists, or well-meaning but sloppy financial managers, the time was now to cash out it seemed. Before it all vanished like fog on a sunny day.

"We need to talk about the offer from Atomic Video Games," Angel whispered.

Lettie knew how excited Angel was about the historically themed video game producer's offer to have him move into a house in Oklahoma City with other content creators and players to shoot a documentary. It was the kind of thing he had dreamed of—a testament to his growing success as a streamer, and they could use the money. But they were new parents, and Lettie couldn't imagine spending two months apart, even if he were less than a two-hour drive away. The move would also mean him dropping out of the online high school they both attended. She didn't mind that idea so much.

"Everything's going so well," Lettie said. "You're the perfect dad. The streaming thing is finally catching. Am I so wrong to want to keep you here? Just enjoy these quiet moments?"

"This could be the start of something bigger. It's my first real break and a chance to get some serious face time with Atomic sponsorship people."

"I get it."

"I won't go if you don't want me to."

"Okay. I don't want you to."

Angel's form remained still, but Lettie sensed something harden within him. Maybe it was the set of his shoulders that rose a little. Maybe it was the firm line of his mouth. Or the way his eyes flashed briefly.

Lettie knew she had just said a very selfish thing. She had her brother and grandmother to help with Milly. Angel's move to Oklahoma City would only be temporary. But after all she had been through, couldn't he understand that she wanted to have things as normal as possible for as long as possible? She tried to soften her words without backing down.

"There will be other opportunities. I know it, Angel. Ones that are closer to home or that come at a better time for us. We're still figuring this parenting thing out."

Angel's jaw flexed, a sign he was irritated with her, but he didn't say anything more. Lettie decided to try a change of topic to restore the contented feeling.

"You know, if we'd taken our payments from your mom's friend in Bitcoin instead of cash, we'd be rich now and you wouldn't even be considering this move. Instead, we blew it on phones and video games. What stupid kids we were, huh?"

She leaned into his shoulder, watching Milly's sweet face as the baby slept. Angel took a deep, sharp breath. His silence was a chilly wall between them. She wanted to push him to argue with her and say what he felt, but she knew by now that when Angel chose to hold back words, he had a reason. She'd just have to wait for the thaw. Surely, he'd see it her way soon. He always did.

She turned back to the laptop, distracting her anxious mind with chatter about hacking a hardware crypto wallet like the one Zane said his client had. The best scenario would be that Zane and Loris find the PIN hidden somewhere in the client's papers or belongings.

Hacking a crypto hardware wallet was a hard thing to do, but not impossible. PINs were usually four or five digits. If it was four digits, that meant mathematically there were only about ten thousand combinations. Child's play for most computers to generate and try. But the wallet would probably only accept a small number of guesses before locking down or destroying the data. So, a brute force hack, where the computer tries every combination, wouldn't work. She watched a video on YouTube about a guy who hacked into a crypto wallet, taking advantage of a weakness in the firmware that allowed him to read the PIN from the device's RAM as it booted up. The hardware manufacturer plugged that hole with a software patch, so it probably wasn't repeatable.

Hearing Angel's deep and even breathing, Lettie grabbed her phone and turned on the camera. She wanted to memorize the sight of him and Milly sleeping, warmed by each other's comfort, so she could call up this feeling of love as soft and warm as summer rain whenever she wanted it. Another photo for the "Daddy Love" album on her phone.

Chapter 5
Zane

That night, Tiffany opened the front door and leaned her flushed face toward him for a kiss. "Ricky just called. The credit card machine at the store isn't working," she said. Her hair was slightly mussed, and she'd wrapped an enormous lime-green scarf around her neck that made her resemble a turtle poking its head out of a shell. "I might have to go back."

"Sure," Zane said. Her intention to go back was clear even though her words were tentative. His role these days was that of an understanding boyfriend who supported her business venture, and he would continue to play it well. But he really hoped there was going to be an end to all these marathon-length days at the store.

"Want me to go with you? Then we can go get dinner at Jason's Deli after if you want."

Her smile was thin, hopeful, and apologetic all at once. "I don't know how long it's going to take," she said, hands on her hips, elbows like barbs against the white doorframe.

"Free soft serve ice cream. It's the best part of Jason's," he

"Something like that. You've heard of it?"

Zane had. There had been a case in Kansas City of a nurse who would administer it to her patients and then "rescue" them from respiratory distress. Awful stuff. It was considered a perfect poison due to the difficulty in detecting it.

"You've never heard of it in any of your studies?"

"No!" Kayla looked shocked as though he had just called her the murderer. "I'm a physical therapist. We work in ice packs and exercises and ultrasound. Not lethal chemicals."

Zane held his hands up in surrender. "I'm just asking what the police are going to ask."

She didn't want to hear that either from the way she gritted her teeth and started to tear apart the tissue in her hands. But to his surprise, she nodded at him. "All right," she said on the intake of her breath, holding herself up. Her tears seemed to recede back into her eyes. "But you're going to help me, aren't you?"

"If I can," he said. "Do they know what time your mother died?"

"Sometime between ten p.m. and one a.m."

He searched for a tactful way to ask what he wanted to ask but came up short. He took the direct approach. "Where were you the night your mother died?"

She answered it just as directly, as though she had decided to get through his suspicion without protest.

"Here. With Tiffany. Watching *Mean Girls* for the millionth time." Her certainty set him back on firm ground; Tiffany he could trust. He would verify it, of course, but this was good news.

It also meant they were looking for more than just a PIN. Now he and Loris were looking for a murderer.

Chapter 6
Zane

Zane sat at his desk in the office at quarter past eight Tuesday morning, drinking a Sour Patch Kids redberry flavored Ghost Energy drink he had picked up at QuikTrip on his way in, his mind hopping around.

First, this redberry flavor was awful. He'd picked it up because the flavor choices were redberry or some bubble gum flavor that sounded terrible, but redberry wasn't any good either. Kind of tasted like battery acid. But it was working. His brain was on high alert.

Second, Tiffany had vouched that she and Kayla had watched *Mean Girls* from ten p.m. to midnight on the night of the murder, and then Kayla had taken a shower and gone to bed afterward. But did Kayla have enough time to drive from Midtown Tulsa to Delaware Pointe to kill her mother after that? Just barely, but it would involve her slipping out of the small apartment unnoticed. Tiffany's video camera doorbell had no video footage of anyone entering or leaving the apartment from nine p.m. until eight the next morning. It didn't seem likely, but Zane wasn't ready to rule it out yet.

Third, how secure could this cryptocurrency be if someone could hire a hacker to get into their wallet? He'd spent a few minutes watching the YouTube videos Lettie had told him about. This guy had lost his password to his digital wallet. After trying a bunch of different ones and only having a few tries left before he was locked out, he hired a hacker to help him get into it. And eventually he did. Zane had a natural skepticism about stories like this. Was it a put-on by these two people for views and likes or whatever? Did they have the password the whole time? Or was this supposedly amazing security actually hackable? Wouldn't that undermine the whole idea of not needing banks to process transactions? It was a head-scratcher for sure.

Fourth, where were the Tulsa police with their investigation into who had killed Dawn Renee? He had done some searching for articles about the crime and found three new stories on news sites. All included photos of the Delaware Pointe house where Dawn had lived, and the same photo Kayla had given him. She must have released it to the media. He read through them all. Dawn Renee's housekeeper found her dead in her bed around nine in the morning. It was a cold and clear night, according to weather reports. No mention of anyone brought in for questioning, no suspects named, only a quote from the Tulsa police communications officer that the investigation was being vigorously pursued.

He took another drink of the Ghost redberry, just to make sure he didn't like it, when the front door to the insurance office swung open. In marched Tulsa Police Detective Angus Pastor, who Zane still thought of as Old Spice because of his old-fashioned aftershave smell.

Loris stood from her chair and watched Old Spice walk through the insurance company's bullpen of desks. A few heads turned. He was a big and burly male with the authoritative stride of a man used to having his questions answered, whether he showed his detective badge or not. Today he was wearing a windbreaker that said TULSA PD in big white letters on the back, so his law enforcement affiliation was more obvious than usual.

When he arrived at the door of Loris Trapper Investigations, Loris spoke. "Good morning, Angus. I didn't know you were coming."

"I'm here to pick up Dawn Renee's phone. Kayla said you had it. I'd have sent someone but when I heard it was you two, I came myself on my way to the station. Why are you two involved with Kayla Renee and her mother's death?"

"Are you asking this officially or as friends?" Loris leaned back in her chair as though blown back by the force of his rat-a-tat questioning.

Old Spice was the picture of seriousness. "Please do not mess around with me. Just tell me what you have."

Zane sank back in his chair, not sure what to say and interested to see how Loris would handle it. She had said many times that what their clients told them was in confidence. But private investigators didn't have the same kind of protections as attorneys, doctors, or priests when it came to keeping things confidential. So, it was a tricky balance. After all, the people who came to private investigators didn't usually want to broadcast their problems.

Loris expelled a breath, slow and loud, like she was in a yoga class. "Someone is in a mood. I'll make it brief. The daughter is our client. We just started on the case."

Old Spice leaned against the door jamb, reflexively patting his shirt pocket where he kept his e-cigarette without taking it out for a puff. "She's got an alibi that checks out for the most part. When did she hire you?"

"The day before you determined it was a murder. We've

got an avenue or two but nothing like a blinking sign flashing," Loris said.

"She was suspicious?"

"Let's just say her mother left her some money but she needs more information in order to collect it. Is there anything you might want to share with us? Anything that hasn't been in the news?" Loris said. "You know we will share if we find anything."

Old Spice snorted at this. "After what you two pulled with Clyde Doom when he escaped from custody, I am very suspicious you'll share any information."

Zane winced at the mention of his half-brother who had escaped from prison hell bent on revenge-killing Zane. That was how Zane met Loris. Clyde had died from a gunshot wound in that standoff—another bombshell on Zane's long list of personal traumas—with the unintended consequence of getting him booted from the police training academy. He felt the old anger coming on but kept it in check. It was never a good idea to get angry at the one person who had supported him.

"That was different," Zane said. "That was personal."

"Yeah, right." Old Spice's brows shot up. "And foolish. But I'll tell you this. If there's money involved, that sounds and smells like motive to me, and you might just want to come clean right now. Or tell her to."

"We'll pass that on," Loris said. "Friendly advice from the local police."

"You should go on a comedy tour," Old Spice said. "This murder was either done by a professional or someone who knew Dawn well. No signs of a break-in or struggle. Like I said, we're not ruling out anyone, even the daughter with her alibi."

Loris's cell trilled its mechanical ring and she glanced at the screen. "Spammer call," she said, flicking the sound off and laying the phone back down.

"Any video evidence?" Zane asked. "Surely they've got cameras all over that neighborhood."

"We're working through it," Old Spice said. "We've got a video showing one person who approached the house on foot. Couldn't see the face."

"Her boyfriend, maybe? Kayla said her mom was seeing someone named Gabriel, but she'd never met him," Loris said.

"Gabriel Connor. He's some kind of freelance computer programmer. Says they were on the outs, and he was playing video games all night online. Seems to check out so far."

Now it was Old Spice's phone shrieking in his pocket. He pulled it out, barked the word "yes" at whoever was on the other end, then said he'd be on his way.

"Thanks, Angus," Loris said. "We'll let you know the minute we find something valuable."

Old Spice snorted as he walked out the door, Dawn Renee's phone in hand. "Sure, take your time. I'll just try to make something useful out of it."

Gabriel Connor sounded like someone who would know his way around a cryptocurrency wallet, so Loris sent Zane to talk to him while she went to inspect a suspicious fire scene for another client. YouTube had a speech Gabriel had made at a computer security forum called Black Hat in California, about how the U.S. government was really governed by a small group of billionaires known as the Star Chamber, not the President or Congress. Gabriel was convincing at the start and unhinged by the end, so Zane wasn't sure what to expect from the conversation.

Zane pulled into the cracked and faded blacktop parking lot of Gabriel's apartment building in the southern end of midtown Tulsa. The rectangular two-story apartment building had a red brick exterior and windows with sagging mini blinds flanked by weathered black shutters. Two wooden columns, white but faded and scratched, held up a wooden overhang that flaked paint like dandruff on the brick walkway. Fluffy green bushes in the planters hadn't been trimmed in a while. A plastic sign staked in an empty planter said, "Please Pick Up After Your Dog." The sign was useless, judging by the volume of doggie waste in the planter. Some old television show's laugh track and the smell of broiling meat wafted out from the adjacent screen door. The Broken Arrow Expressway was so close Zane could just about read the license plates of trucks whooshing by.

The building didn't have a lobby, with apartment front doors facing the parking lot. Direct access was helpful. Zane banged on the metal edge of the screen door for apartment 121 —Gabriel's number. The wooden door behind it creaked open to reveal the face of the hacker, now older of course, from the video Zane had found. He was a tall, pale man in black jeans and a black T-shirt that read "RUN CMD c:\>_." Lettie would have known right away what the T-shirt meant. He was a few inches taller than Zane and peered down at him, wary as a coyote on the prowl. His face even had a canine element, long-nosed, round eyes set far apart, thin lips set in a half-smile. Behind him, Zane could see a bank of computer screens with green code running like in *The Matrix*.

Gabriel studied Zane's business card like it had secret lottery numbers embedded in it for long enough that Zane began to suspect he was high. Zane could just detect the faint but skunky smell of marijuana on him.

"What can I tell you that I haven't already told the police? I met Dawn online last year and we hung out a lot for a while but then she pushed the stop button. That's it. I hadn't even talked to her since March."

His cold manner was giving Zane all the wrong feels. He couldn't imagine learning that anyone he had been close to was murdered and reacting without some shock or horror. Gabriel twitched and shifted like a cat caught by the tail. He was blocking the door, clearly not going to let Zane inside, and seemed to be threatening with every moment to slam the door shut. Zane decided to play his best card.

"What do you know about the million bucks in crypto on the hard wallet she left behind?"

That got a reaction. Gabriel stopped twitching and leaned forward, mouth open to reveal rabbity, butter-yellow teeth. "Sounds like a smart investment by a smart woman."

"Her daughter found it but can't find the PIN to access it. Do you know anything about that?"

A short, barking laugh broke from his chest. "Good luck with that," Gabriel said. "That's a tough problem to solve. Is that why you're here?"

Zane speared him with a mean glare. "Dawn's daughter has been through a lot. You could have some sympathy."

"I never met her." He shrugged his narrow shoulders as though he couldn't be expected to relate to a young woman who just found out her mother was murdered. "If that's all, I've got to get back to something."

It wasn't a question, so Zane didn't answer it. "Call me if you think of anything that could help," he said but Gabriel was already closing the door before he could finish. What a jerk.

Chapter 7
Zane

A pristine white cement driveway, a good quarter mile long and straight as a sunbeam, led to a huge two-story wedding-cake house. The office of Terry Pickert Real Estate Development was in a massive mansion on the outskirts of the Delaware Pointe neighborhood in Broken Arrow. To Zane, the house looked like a tornado had lifted it from some estate in Europe and tossed it down in the middle of the prairie, next to flat, dusty parcels of land waiting to be turned into new homes.

Judging from the size, the furniture inside, and the friendliness of the receptionist, the company, and probably the home-building industry, was doing just fine despite inflation. Zane and Loris had to wait twenty minutes to get in to see Terry Pickert, though he had told Kayla he was happy to help her in any way and that included talking to the detectives she hired.

Pickert stood in a shaft of mid-morning sunlight, looking out his office window when Zane and Loris finally got inside. The real estate developer and his office were perfectly matched. The room was big and opulent, and so was Pickert, in a tailored suit that fit him perfectly and an orangey-pink shirt that nearly matched his inflated, ruddy complexion. Of medium height with fair hair making a slow retreat away from his forehead, he had the look of a man who drank and ate too much, and the excess pounds had given him a wide neck that made the collar of his shirt look tight. He shook both their hands with a politician's lingering eye contact and said he was happy to help Kayla but had no idea how he could. He gestured at two chairs in front of the desk, the friendly expression morphing into something more wary.

"We're detectives," Loris said, sliding a business card over the large wooden desk to Pickert. "Kayla hired us to find out who killed her mother."

Pickert cocked his head and drummed his fingers on the desk for a moment. "I just heard about that. It's crazy. Do you think it could have been a random crime, like a serial killer? Or was someone targeting her in particular?"

"We're keeping an open mind," Zane said.

"But Kayla says she has a feeling there's more to the story and that's what she hired us to find out," Loris added. "She made a list of names of the people her mother had contact with and doesn't see how it could be any of them. She has started thinking it must be someone she doesn't know about. Maybe someone connected to her work here, or someone from her mother's past. That's why we wanted to start with you. She worked here, and you knew her—how long?"

"More than two decades." He chewed on his lower lip a moment. "You seem like you think it might be someone in this organization, and I can't even imagine that. We're like a family here. A dysfunctional family sometimes, sure, but we get along. We're professionals. Right now, I've got twenty-three people on the payroll. Over the two decades Dawn worked here, we've probably had eighty-one or so. At the risk of sounding naïve, I can't imagine any one of them with a motivation to murder Dawn. Maybe that's what people always say only to be proven wrong later. Because who knows what beats in the heart of men, right? But I mean it."

"Maybe you can give us a list anyway," Loris said.

"Sure. The Tulsa Police covered this ground too, about two hours ago. We put the list together for them so we can let you have a copy. But I think you're wasting your time."

"Thanks. Now can we go through some dates? When did Dawn start working for you?"

Zane opened up his notebook.

"I looked that up for the police as well. It was August 14, 2002."

"Did you know her before then?"

"No. She came by the office to drop off her resume. We had run an ad on one of those online websites—I remember because it had such a silly name, like MonsterJobs?—and she came in person and asked to see me and hand deliver it. I liked her verve. I only had two other people working for me back then out of a model home in a little subdivision called Barrett Ridge I was building in Jenks. We were doing a realtor tour that day and our computer network had crashed. We were trying to get our IT consultant on the phone, and Dawn asked if she could help. I said sure and she jumped right in. Twenty minutes later, the network was back up. I hired her that day."

"Where had she worked before?"

"I don't remember. Something in IT. It's funny. After she died, I looked in her personnel file for that resume. Couldn't find it."

"Do you remember calling her references or anything when you hired her?"

"I didn't need to call her references. I could see with my own eyes how good she was."

Zane rested the pen in the open spine of his notebook. "She never said anything about where she worked before? In all that time you worked with her?"

Pickert shook his head. "What can I tell you? It's a busy office and she was a private person. I didn't think much of it."

"Tell us about the trip she took to Fort Worth last month."

Pickert's pursed lips widened, then tilted up in one corner like Loris's question had unlocked a core memory. "I forgot about that," he said. "The Fort Worth development. What a fiasco." A bittersweet smile appeared on his face. "Where did you hear about that?"

"Kayla remembered it. Says her mother was very upset about having to go but you insisted." Loris studied Pickert like she was looking for her favorite song on the jukebox. Zane knew she was searching for indications of increased stress that might give them some ideas where to investigate further. At the police academy, they had been taught to watch for groups of signs: someone who crosses their arms, turns their head, moves their feet all at once. But Pickert didn't shift his position.

Pickert flicked his eyes between Zane and Loris, still smiling that sad smile. "It was strange. To me, it seemed like a routine request, go down to Fort Worth and set up the network for a development I was a partner in. Granted, this is my first development outside the greater Tulsa area, but it's only a five-hour drive, and I thought she'd enjoy getting out of town. I even told her she could make a weekend out of it, see the stockyards or the zoo or something. But Dawn was downright livid. How dare I ask her to do such a thing? It was the most emotion I'd ever seen come out of her."

"Why was she upset about it? Did she say?"

"She didn't say."

"That seems surprising given how emotional you said she

was," Zane said. "You didn't ask why she was upset about going to Fort Worth?"

Now Pickert leaned forward, holding his hands up as though in surrender. "Dawn was a private person. And I suppose I'm not a very curious boss."

As the real estate developer admitted to being clueless about his own employee's private life, Zane quickly realized that the supposed "family atmosphere" at Pickert Real Estate was nothing but a facade. Pickert's demeanor was cold and calculating as he continued speaking.

"Look, as long as the work is getting done, I don't care. I'm not here to be friends and give hugs. I told her if she didn't go, then she was out of the job. I wasn't bluffing either. She knew it and she went. She wasn't happy about it, but she understood I was the boss and I needed her there. If you want to know more about that Fort Worth trip, talk to Martina Decomo. She is my head of sales, and she was on that trip with Dawn. She's sharper than me in about a hundred ways, so maybe her memory will be better."

He picked up his cell phone and sent a text. Pickert was all business now, ready to end the interview by pushing them over to this Martina Decomo. But the text notification dinged, and he pressed his lips together. "She's at the dentist's. I can have her give you a call when she's done." He stood up, stepped around the desk, and held out his hand. "Nice to meet you both. We'll help you as much as we can, but I need to get back to work." His handshake was brisk and firm.

Loris wasn't done though. "So where were you the night she died?"

Pickert screwed his face up like he was sucking on a lemon. "I was with my family, packing to go to our house in Branson for the weekend."

"We're just trying to eliminate you as a suspect," she said.

Pickert rolled his eyes then turned his attention back to his phone as they departed.

Loris left to meet another client for lunch, so Zane went home to the Majestic Mobile Home and RV Park to see Lettie and eat some of Verda's cooking. His grandmother had bought the three-bedroom doublewide mobile home. She decided to come live with them after they found out Lettie was pregnant last year. It sat just a stone's throw from the lot where he and Lettie had lived with their mother, who died in a fire there two years ago. A new family lived in that space now, bikes and toys littering the ground around the home and the rose bush he and Lettie had planted in memorial to her.

Verda had made the new mobile home cozy and welcoming inside, but outside it still looked like a fortress. The security cameras and floodlights installed at each corner were an ever-present reminder of the dark storm that had been his half-brother, Clyde Doom. At least the ridiculous bear trap was gone. Zane blinked his eyes to try to clear the mental image of Clyde's face, snarled in anger like the wolf in his bad neck tattoo.

Two years ago, Zane's life had been turned upside down by his mother's death and his ill-fated search for his father, Jeremiah Doom with lasting consequences. Clyde had escaped from prison and come after Zane seeking revenge, blowing up Zane's chance at becoming a police officer. And now Clyde was dead too, shot in self-defense by Verda. If Zane's life so far had been a cycle and recycle through violence and fear, he was breaking that cycle one day at a time.

Did he have regrets about looking for his father after his mother's death? Yes. That act had led him to the dangerous Dooms and their casual violence. But his search for truth had felt inevitable, just as Kayla Renee must be feeling. Before his mother died and in the aftermath of her death, he had felt deeply empty. Not knowing your father created one hell of a psychological black hole. He had thought he would fill it up by finding his dad. That had not worked. He knew now that the way to fill it up was through the love of his sister, his grandmother, his niece, and Tiffany. And by helping people. Like they say in Alcoholics Anonymous, the best way out of the garbage thoughts in your head was to be of service to someone else. Which is what he was going to do for Kayla. Maybe that million dollars in cryptocurrency would help her start a new life.

The sounds of whining and the jangle of dog tags on a collar came from behind the front door. Zane opened it against the weight of Ballpoint leaning into it, so eager to see him that the pit bull wouldn't retreat to let him into the house. Zane gently pushed him back so he could get inside. As he crossed to dump his keys on the dining table, Ballpoint followed close behind, panting heavily, his entire back-end wiggling in frantic welcome, as if it were about to break loose from the rest of his body. Zane loved this dog—Ballpoint had turned out to be the best part of the whole Clyde Doom episode—but he hadn't realized what a full-time job dog ownership was. Vet bills, trips outside to "do his business," the drumbeat of daily meals and walks. But when the pit bull gazed up at him with moist, adoring eyes, Zane pretty much melted every time. He knelt to scratch the back of the dog's neck.

"Zane?" Verda called from the kitchen. "Are you home?"

"I'm here," Zane said. He continued rubbing the soft velvet on top of Ballpoint's head. Two dirty-looking storage bins had appeared in the living room along with a stack of hardback books. Just as Zane still battled to stay sober every day, Verda fought and sometimes gave in to her hoarding tendencies with her regular trips to the thrift store. Lettie, Angel, and Zane tag-teamed to keep the junk at bay, often sneaking her finds out to the dumpster after she went to sleep. Looks like they had another load to deal with. But Verda had been getting wise to them lately, stashing things in her room, which they considered off-limits.

He shifted his attention to the television set, which was tuned to "Judge Judy," a blonde, washed-out looking woman with small eyes holding up a sheet of paper.

"I've got a real treat," Verda said, while Judge Judy started lecturing the woman. "I've made Frito pie."

Zane brightened considerably at the mention. As he walked toward the kitchen, the chili-and-corn-chip smell tempted him to eat straight out of the casserole dish. But Verda would hate that. He sat at down at the table while Verda poured tall glasses of iced tea as sparkly as Ballpoint's eyes.

"So, what have you been doing all morning?" Verda said, spooning Frito pie into two bowls for them. His grandmother was sixty-three years old, with a soft, round, pretty face. When Zane first met her after his mother's death, she had been soft and round all over, using a cane for stability, but the last year he'd seen her transform herself, losing weight and taking daily walks. She was caring, compassionate, sweet, and as good with guns as she was at cooking. He had no idea how she didn't put the weight back on with all the cooking she did. He had certainly gained a few pounds.

"Had a visit from our favorite detective," Zane said. "Turns out our cryptocurrency case is now a murder." He filled Verda in on the basics of the case without divulging more than she could find in the news.

"You think they killed her for the million dollars in crypto?"

Zane looked up to see Lettie holding Milly. He stood up to hug his sister and kiss the baby's fat cheek. That familiar feeling of family and love swept through him like a warm wave. He tried to draw the feeling around him like a quilt, but like all feelings—good or bad—it evaporated like the details of a dream. By the end of his next exhale, Milly was protesting in her mama's arms. This week's baby drama was Milly's flare-up of diaper rash. She still seemed uncomfortable despite two days of layering zinc oxide cream like frosting on her tiny bottom.

The next moment, Milly was in Verda's arms, head resting against her great-grandmother's chin. Verda was stroking the back of her head and whispering to her that she was the most wonderful girl in the world. Outside, an April wind gust shook the mobile home, making Zane feel cozy and content inside its walls surrounded by his family, the room fitting the four of them snugly.

"Money makes people do crazy things," Verda said.

"Do I get a finder's fee if you get into that wallet?" Lettie asked.

"You get free room and board, smart aleck. Why don't you tell me what you know about cryptocurrency wallets?" Zane said.

"Other than to scam people, I don't know why people are inventing new ways to have money when the old way works fine," Verda said. "Give me dollar bills any time. You want anonymity? Pay in cash."

"You have a point," Lettie said. Seconds later, Milly was wailing. She reached for her mama, her cries intensifying. Lettie took her as the baby threw her head back and howled. "I'll nurse her," Lettie said, raising her voice to be heard over the cries.

Verda sank into a chair, and they sat quietly for a moment, chewing Frito pie, and drinking tea while Milly settled into a quiet rhythm on her mother's breast.

"If you want, I can check the firmware version on the wallet," Lettie said. Getting three sets of blank looks, she explained. "Firmware is permanent software programmed into a read-only memory. Basically, it provides instructions to the machine. It's important here because most of the success stories of hacking into these types of wallets has to do with a hole in the firmware code that allows people to see the PIN when you start-up the wallet."

"So, it can be done?" Zane said.

"I don't know yet. Let me see it. It may be beyond my skills."

"You know if Lettie says something is beyond her skills, it must be hard," Zane said to Verda, his voice taking on just the slightest edge from the ongoing stress of trying to raise his teenage sister. Even with his grandmother's help, it was a challenge to keep Lettie on track sometimes. Lately she had been talking about dropping out of high school and getting her GED instead. She didn't even seem interested in going to college. "She tells me she knows everything." Verda shook her head at Zane, indicating he had gone too far.

A flicker of annoyance went over Lettie's face, a remnant of their last argument about finishing school.

"Your best bet is to find that PIN. It's going to be a four- or five-digit number," Lettie said.

"Even with all this computer nonsense, it comes down to finding a slip of paper with numbers on it," Verda said. "The more things change, the more things stay the same."

But before Zane could open his mouth to start talking about possible hiding places for such a number, someone was knocking on the front door. Verda's manner changed. Her grandmotherly countenance disappeared. Now she seemed younger, excited, smoothing her hair behind her ears and smiling broadly.

Zane opened the door to see his grandmother's boyfriend outside. About the same age as Verda, Leon Garcia was lanky with thick salt-and-pepper hair, side-parted and glistening.

Old-fashioned hair cream froze his comb-tracks in place like the grooves on a vinyl record. He'd picked his hairstyle sometime in the 1970s and never looked back.

Leon rubbed his left shoulder reflexively when he saw Zane, as though trying to erase the bullet wound he'd acquired during the showdown with Clyde Doom. The awkwardness between them had lessened but not vanished since that whole mess. Leon had played both sides of that conflict and almost gotten Zane killed. Verda had found her way to forgive him, and Zane had as well, in a small way. But that didn't mean that letting the man into their home was any easier.

He could see the same reaction on Lettie's face as well. When someone shows you that they're good at lying and sneaking around, it's hard to trust them, even when they wind up doing the right thing.

"Hello everyone," Leon said. He crossed over to where Verda sat, the nylon of his blue windbreaker making a soft shushing noise as his arms reached to squeeze her shoulders. He planted a kiss on her cheek. Zane looked at the roundness of his face, smiling so warmly at Verda, and thought about how Leon lit up when he saw her. As though the fact that she stayed in his life surprised and delighted him every time he saw her. Like he didn't deserve it—which he didn't. But blessings were blessings. No one earned them.

Leon stood behind Verda with his hands on her shoulders. "Did I interrupt something?"

"We're just talking about a case," Zane said. Curiosity lit up Leon's face, but he seemed to think twice about asking for more information. A sign of good sense, Zane thought, since no one in this room other than Verda trusted him.

"Where's Angel?" Leon asked instead.

"He's at the Atomic Video Games office for some meeting," Lettie said. "Like always."

Zane came up with his own excuse to leave. He didn't feel like spending time with Leon, and he thought Lettie might feel the same way.

"It sounds like I need to get your eyes on the hard wallet so you can check out this firmware thing, Lettie," Zane said. "Can you come to the office to look at it? I'd rather not have it out of the safe for too long."

"I could use a field trip," Lettie said. "Do you want to do it now?"

"Sure," Zane said.

They left Milly in the care of Verda and Leon and drove back to the office. By two-thirty, they had driven the six miles to midtown, the drive lengthened by a crash on Interstate 44. Lettie had changed into jeans, a turtleneck, and tennis shoes for the occasion and pulled a dark grey beanie over her hair. In the car, she zoned out. Whatever energy the outing had produced drained away as they drove, and she fell asleep against the passenger window. Zane felt some sympathy for her. Caring for Milly was an act of love but also a marathon and a sprint at the same time.

"We're here," Zane said softly, not wanting to startle her.

Lettie jerked awake. The afternoon was slightly chilly, with a haze in the air. Trees beginning to sprout green bent gracefully in a gust of wind. April in Oklahoma was a mix of stormy and mild days, as likely to drop a hailstorm as a picture-perfect spring day. Today's weather with its cool wind and gauzy mist seemed to straddle the line between the extremes.

They entered the office, Lettie trailing behind him, taking in the rows of tidy desks, all unoccupied but one. A trim and balding man sat there, talking loudly into a phone sandwiched between his wide shoulders and sharp jawline. "I can't spare you any more time!" he said, his voice arcing. A pause, and then, "I'm on a juice fast."

Lettie caught Zane's eye as they entered Loris' office and made a surprised face at the man's revelation. She sat upright in one of the visitors' chairs and drew her laptop out of her bag. "Let's see what you've got." She rubbed her eyes with a knuckle on her right hand.

Zane shut the door and twisted the blinds shut on the interior window looking out into the office. Then he went to the safe at the back of the room, spun the dials, and brought the little black shield-shaped device over to his sister. Lettie held the small device in one hand and ran her fingers over the engraved lettering of the Trezor logo along the top.

"The buttons and no touchscreen mean this is Model One. That's good. It's the first model developed by this company. You can connect it to mobile phones and computers with a cable. It's sort of the grandpa of the hard wallet set. And this is a model that people have hacked successfully."

"Can you tell if it has the version of the—" Zane hesitated, trying to remember the right word "—firmware? The firmware you said people had successfully hacked into."

Lettie snorted. "I didn't mean I could tell by literally looking at it. Do we have the mother's computer or laptop where she connected this wallet? Typically, people manage these wallets through an interface on their computer. That would be step one."

"Oh. Did not know that. Yes, there was a laptop, but I'm sure the police have it now," Zane said. "Maybe her work computer. They might still have it at the office."

Lettie studied the device for a few more seconds then smiled with equal parts hope and discouragement. "Good. That all might help. But here's the bad news. A security feature of the wallet is that if you try the password and get it wrong too many times, it erases the drive. I truly don't want to just mess around with it."

They talked a little bit more about the wallet, and Lettie showed him another one of the videos of a hacker taking apart the Trezor wallet to hack into the microchip inside.

"I thought you just tapped into the keyboard or something to do the hacking," Zane said.

"That's how they show it in the movies," Lettie said. "But sometimes the goal is to push hardware beyond its intended use. That's a skill I haven't mastered."

"So, we're back to good old-fashioned legwork. We need to find that PIN," Zane said.

"That's your best bet," Lettie said.

Chapter 8
Lettie

After a short day of online high school, Lettie took Milly to the new playground at Majestic Mobile Home and RV Park. It was just after lunch when they strolled down the park road. She had basically lived her whole life at the Majestic, except for the year spent in the apartment with Zane. Even though the day was overcast, the old trailer park looked better than ever, green buds emerging on bare branches, green grass shooting its way past bleached white winter blades. A few of the old neighbors were still around, like Emmaline and her parents and Mrs. Ahern, and the new neighbors were kind to her and Milly, offering babysitting and hand-me-down clothes. She liked her life as it was, and Angel wanted to change all of that with his opportunity in Oklahoma City. It was frustrating to have to negotiate with him to get what she wanted. Maybe this was why some people just stayed single. She thought about asking Emmaline for advice.

Emmaline Perryman was the closest thing she had to an older sister. She was twenty-seven, like Zane, a wannabe reality television star and influencer whose main source of income was making show-stopping dresses for pageant queens of all ages—from tiny tots to teenagers. She ran her sewing studio out of her parents' mobile home where she also lived. She had gone to Los Angeles last year to try to make it, but an abusive boyfriend and lack of opportunities brought her back home. She was a very beautiful woman: a bit taller than Lettie, lean and spray-tanned, her dark hair dyed a golden California blonde that looked as shiny as a polished car. She'd always treated Lettie with respect and affection, but she had also broken Zane's heart more than once. She seemed to cast spells over men, though Zane had finally broken the enchantment for good. It shouldn't have surprised her to find Emmaline walking hand-in-hand with some new dude when she pushed Milly by the Perrymans' driveway.

The Perrymans' home faced a picturesque little bit of scenery in one of the trailer park's open spaces. A weeping willow and three rosebushes sat on the edge of a patch of grass slowly turning green.

"Lettie! Milly! Come over here. There's someone I want you to meet," Emmaline said, breaking out into a fast walk toward her with the man trailing behind her.

He must have been in his thirties, slightly plump, with a crown of tight brown curls. He was struggling to grow a mustache that only made him look like a fugitive. But it was his eyes that bothered her most: icy-blue, small, and just for a moment, venomous. Lettie had seen husbands on that television show *Dateline* she would trust before him.

Emmaline dragged him to the edge of the driveway and bent to give Milly a kiss. "This is Guy Callahan," she said, then nodded at her. "My sister from another mother, Lettie Magdite. Guy moved here from San Diego. He's renting a room from Mrs. Ahern."

Guy held out a hand to shake hers. It was limp and damp,

but Lettie smiled sociably. His return smile erased the chill from his gaze, and she found herself doing a mental doubletake, wondering if it had been a trick of the light.

"Welcome to the neighborhood," she said. "So, you're from San Diego?"

"Oh, I'm not from anywhere really," Guy said, glancing from the corners of his eyes at Emmaline. "I've lived in lots of places, but yeah, most recently San Diego. I wasn't sure how long I'd stay in Tulsa, but Miss Emmaline makes it very welcoming."

He wore a white T-shirt under an open button-down shirt with a bright orange and pink geometric print. The T-shirt stretched tight over a rounded belly, not unlike a partially deflated soccer ball. His excess weight was carried in his chest, arms, and waist, stacked on long skinny legs. He wore scuffed black combat boots and a huge stainless-steel watch that looked big enough to use as a wall clock. Lettie finished taking his measure and wanted to make eye contact again, but he ducked over Milly and started babbling.

"Aren't you just a sweetie pie? Aren't you just?" Guy said to Milly.

Milly's mouth came open in a cry so deep-seated she made no sound at first. She curled her body inward while she gathered her strength and then howled at her highest pitch. Guy backed off like Milly had tried to bite him.

Lettie pushed the stroller forward and back, hoping to soothe her with the motion and a few "there, there's." Apparently, her baby didn't like Guy any more than she did. But Emmaline didn't seem to notice. Her eyes flicked between Guy and Milly.

"Isn't she beautiful?" Emmaline said, her eyes big.

"Maybe when she's not crying," Guy said.

"You're so funny." She laughed effusively and pushed at his

arm, an over-the-top reaction for such a basic wisecrack. Lettie was not impressed by him, and she was sure he sensed it. She wasn't an extrovert, but she did like most people as a rule. Most were kind and interesting if you got to know them. But something was off with Guy: he was calculating and fake. And she was pretty sure he didn't like her either.

"Do you want to come in for some lunch?" Emmaline said, gesturing toward her parents' home. "I can show you the Easter dress I'm making for little Milly. It's almost done. You're going to love it. And we're about to go make some toasted cheese sandwiches. Guy here aims to give me a soft life."

"You deserve it, baby," he said.

Lettie could feel her face set with discomfort, watching them paw at each other for a moment. He seemed so fake. Bad flashbacks of Emmaline and that tool she had hooked up with in Los Angeles came to her like this was déjà vu. When would she learn how to pick a good guy? It was like honest and kind men were invisible to her.

"Naw, I'm just going to take Milly over to the playground. Gotta get some of that vitamin D while there's a chance of sun," she said. "I'll come by to see the dress later, okay?" The comment about the sun was a lie: the sky was a low ceiling of white clouds. But the two lovebirds didn't seem to notice.

Lettie pushed the stroller over the bumpy pea gravel that encircled the mobile home park's playground. Two toddlers stabbed at the sand in the sand box with plastic shovels while two women at least ten years older than Lettie sat on the nearby bench talking. They looked up at her and smiled in unison, but she couldn't shake the feeling that they were talking about her. Wondering how old she was. Wondering why she wasn't in school. Teen mom-land was full of ostracism. People her own age avoided her like pregnancy was contagious. The older moms with babies steered clear too, not sure if she was the babysitter or sister. She maneuvered the stroller around some dog poop and watched Milly kick her legs at the air.

"You going to be a soccer player, little one?" she said. Milly was four months old, and she was starting to hold her head and back steadily and taking more interest in her surroundings. Lettie pointed the stroller at the kids in the sandbox and Milly watched them with contentment. Lettie took out her phone and shot a quick video of Milly, eyes wide and alert, waving her arm at the camera. She sent it in a message to Angel. His response came fast: *Adorable!*

Then: *Atomic says I have to a week to decide about Oklahoma City.*

She started typing a response, *Tell them no today,* then deleted it. She stood staring at the phone screen for a few more moments. Then she slipped the phone in her pocket without responding. Was he serious about this OKC thing after she told him how she felt? She turned her attention to Milly, lifted her out of the stroller, and carried her over to the sandbox. She sat on the cool sand with Milly in between her legs and let her grab sand in her hand. The two toddlers continued to bury some toy cars in the sand, ignoring them just as she ignored the new notification on her phone, probably from Angel.

Chapter 9
Zane

Martina Decomo was in her early forties and curvy, wearing an apricot blouse and white pants. Zane didn't know much about women's clothes, but it seemed like she was dressing for a balmy spring climate that Tulsa weather was not delivering this Wednesday afternoon. She was an alpha boss type with big dark eyes and a shark's smile made more intimidating somehow by her slight overbite, toothy and ready to nip. She had a salesperson's practiced friendliness and even tone. She'd offered to come to Loris' office to talk. Zane hoped that meant that she had information to share that she didn't want others in Pickert's office to hear. But Martina dispelled that idea with her first statement.

"I live right around the corner from here so I'm going straight home for the day after this. Never been in this building before," she said, sizing up their room filled with three desks and a flank of filing cabinets. "A sublease or something?"

"I do a lot of work for the insurance company, so they let me have the space as part of my compensation," Loris said.

A strong floral perfume oozed off Martina. "Terry said you

have some questions about Dawn Renee. I just can't believe it. Murder, they're saying. Terrible thing. Just terrible."

"How well did you know her?"

"Not very well. We worked together, gosh, for fifteen years, I think. She was already working for Pickert when I started." Martina reached for her phone and looked at a notification that had popped up on the screen with a ding. Whatever it was, it wasn't that important because she let her hand holding the phone drop to her thigh and cleared her throat. "What sort of information are you looking for?"

"Whatever you can tell us," Loris said. "Dawn's daughter Kayla hired us to see if we can help find her killer. We thought we'd start with her work."

"Why me first?"

Zane told her about Kayla's memory of the Fort Worth trip and Pickert's suggestion that she might remember the source of Dawn's reluctance. Martina's manner seemed to shift, becoming less wary. She slid the Prada sunglasses off the top of her head and twirled them in a tight circle by the end. She was a woman who valued appearances, Zane thought, given the way she dressed and carried herself. Someone who believed that you only had one chance to make a first impression. And the impression she gave was one of success. The sunglass twirling seemed reckless, as though the glasses might break free and fly across the room, making it hard to concentrate on what she was saying: "Talking to Dawn was like trying to convince a brick wall to share its life story. In sales, we call these folks "cold fish" - tough to reel in and even harder to connect with."

Loris switched tactics suddenly, maybe to throw her off-balance. "When did you see her last?"

Martina stopped twirling the sunglasses. "I guess it was the afternoon of the night she died. I'd left at the usual time. Took my laptop and stuff to work from home after dinner, like I usually do. I wasn't like Dawn, sticking around the office late at night. Terry knows I'll make myself available at night if I need to, but my priority is to be home with my girls. They're five and seven."

"You were with your family all night that night?" Loris asked.

Martina's head went back, and she laughed good and loud. "You think I killed her? I barely knew her and that's saying something when you work with someone for fifteen years. Look, I know you're not supposed to speak badly of the dead, but this was a woman who lived, breathed, and ate work. That's all there was to her. Her daughter was an afterthought. Dawn would say she was raising Kayla to be independent but to me it looked like neglect. I thought something was wrong with her."

"Why didn't she want to go on that trip?"

"Leaving her grown daughter in Tulsa wasn't the problem. It was Fort Worth that had Dawn hesitant."

"So, what was it?"

"I think it was a man who lived in Fort Worth."

"How do you know that? Did she tell you?" Zane asked.

"She didn't have to tell me. I saw it firsthand. We were at a restaurant in Fort Worth. I convinced her that we deserved a fancy night out, courtesy of Terry, so I found the nearest five-star. A place called The Bull Farmhouse if you're interested. We're not seated ten minutes before this older man comes up to us. Custom-made suit, huge watch that must have set him back seven thousand dollars on his wrist, the genteel manners of an old man from the south. He must have been in his seventies, I'd guess. What we'd call a 'white whale' in sales. Rich, elusive, very rare. I took notice."

She paused, watching Zane as he scratched down the description in his notebook.

"I expected a come-on, but his vibe was fatherly. Maybe

even grandfatherly. Old Dawn, though, the blood drained from her face like he was a vampire. She looked shocked. She couldn't move him away from our table fast enough. But I was in full sales mode. She may have been in Fort Worth for computer nerd stuff, but I was there to sell homes. I introduce myself, hand him a card and tell him if he is looking for some real estate investments to give me a call. He told me his name was Sherwood Rittenhour. I did a Google search on him later. My hunch had been correct. He was loaded. Founded some telecommunications company out there."

From Martina's face, Zane might have thought she was telling a story that happened yesterday, not a month ago. Clearly, this Sherwood Rittenhour made a lasting impression.

"Did you tell the police all this?" Zane asked.

"No. I mean, no one from the police has even talked to me yet. Anyway, this man didn't seem to want to harm her. He wanted to, I don't know, hug her or something."

"But you said she had a weird reaction to him, right? The blood drained from her face?" Loris repeated Martina's words back to her. "Was she scared of him?"

Martina cocked her head and squinted her eyes as though trying to peer around the corner at a memory. "Scared isn't the word. She was upset. Angry-sad if that's a thing. She did not want to talk to him, and she didn't want me to talk to him either. In the middle of the conversation, her phone rang, and she just ignored it. I said, 'Maybe you should get that. It could be your daughter,' and you would have thought I stabbed her in the heart." Her smile turned shark-like again. "She got up and ran out. Left me sitting there. When she left, he turned to me and asked how old her daughter was. I told him she was in her twenties. Then he asked me how I knew Dawn, and I told him that we worked together at Pickert. He excused himself and returned to his table. He was sitting with some guy, probably a flunky or something. I sat there like a chump and drank a thirty-dollar glass of pinot by myself and waited for her to come back. She never did. I wound up eating by myself at the bar. Next day, she didn't say a word about it other than a simple apology. I asked her who he was to her, but she just shook her head. Didn't even try to make up an answer. Just said nothing. She was like that sometimes, stony cold."

"She never said anything else about him?" Loris asked.

"Not to me. Lord knows I tried to pump her about him, but she was a weird one. One of the few people I know who you could ask a direct question and she just plain wouldn't answer you. Later, I started to wonder if he was the baby daddy. I mean, imagination jumps in to fill a vacuum, right?"

"Did she have any other friends at the office? Or enemies?"

"Not that I can think of. She really kept to herself." Martina shook her head for emphasis. The gesture turned into a neck roll, complete with cracking noises. "Sorry about that. I'm overdue for an adjustment at the chiropractor. Anyway, that's all I know. I'm sorry if it's not more helpful. Terry said we should all cooperate. He sent out an email."

"Kayla told us he didn't use email," Zane said.

A smile formed on Martina's lips, and she leaned forward as though telling a secret. "Correction. Pickert's assistant sent out an email. She ghostwrites all his emails. I don't think he knows how to click a mouse. She prints his emails for him to read on paper. Can you believe it?"

Martina sat expectantly in the chair for a few more beats. She was enjoying her turn in the spotlight of this investigation, Zane could tell. He could also sense that Loris was getting antsy too. The Sherwood Rittenhour lead was tantalizing, and she'd probably want to start digging into his back story before the day was over. An older, wealthy man with a technical background was an intriguing lead.

After a few more fruitless questions about Dawn's background, Martina checked her phone and rose from the chair to leave, but not before laying a stack of her business cards on the corner of Loris' desk. "In case you know anyone looking to get in a brand-new home," she said.

Zane watched her walk out of the office building, but not before leaving another stack of her cards on the reception desk of the insurance office. He'd heard the salesperson's mantra "always be closing" somewhere and found himself repeating it as she exited.

"All right, let's start learning everything we can about Sherwood Rittenhour," Loris said but Zane was already feeding the name into the mouth of the mighty Internet. An hour later, they knew enough about Sherwood Rittenhour to fill a dozen pages. But Zane wasn't sure how much of it would prove useful. For example, did it matter that he collected spears and other weaponry from Micronesia and Polynesia? Probably only to the Pacific islanders he bought the objects from on one of his adventure tours to the area. A few things had surfaced that seemed pertinent. His grandfather had built a fancy mansion back in the 1930s in Fort Worth's exclusive Westover Hills area that Rittenhour still lived in. Family money came from the bank Grandpa Rittenhour founded. Prosperity Financial Bank catered to the oilmen who came in droves in search of black gold in the early part of the twentieth century. Rittenhour had ambitions beyond the family bank, though. He founded Worth-Comm with a college roommate and grew it into a behemoth.

Rittenhour only married one time and she died in 2010. He had one daughter, Caroline, who lived in Atlanta with her husband and was an economics professor at Emory University, and a son, named Curtis, fifty years old, vice president of Prosperity Financial Bank. Rittenhour was a member of seven boards of directors, including Prosperity Financial Bank and the Internet Society which aimed to spread the joys of the Internet around the globe. Zane had noted with interest Rittenhour's appearance as an advisor to the Global Blockchain Business Council because blockchain was a word somehow related to cryptocurrency. Zane knew that much, but he wasn't about to admit he didn't understand the connection exactly.

"What's the approach?" Zane asked. "Do we just call him and ask to talk? Should we go to Fort Worth? I know you said it's always better to do things in person."

"This one's tricky," Loris said. "If we call and are upfront about what we want, there's a good chance he will ignore us. I know these corporate bigwig types. They've got a stable of people ready to run interference for them. I think we're going to have to use a bit of subterfuge. What do you know about him after all that research?"

He showed Loris what he had, even throwing in the Polynesian spear collection for good measure.

To his surprise, that was the item she landed on as most interesting.

"That's it," Loris said. She pointed on the screen at a photo essay of three rooms in Rittenhour's mansion devoted to the spears, masks, necklaces, headdresses, and oars of the Micronesian people. "One of the finest collections of Pacific Islander art and objects. That's how we'll get to him."

After another twenty minutes of Internet searching, they realized it would take a lot more work to be able to credibly talk about this art to a connoisseur like Rittenhour. So, they took a shortcut, searching for a piece of Oceanic art that was very rare, and landed on a museum piece that would sound irresistible to a collector if it were for sale. Rittenhour wouldn't be able to refuse the prospect.

It took three people to get Loris and Zane's call through to Rittenhour's office at WorthComm, where he still held the title chairman of the board at age seventy-three. First, one of those automated messages telling you to press one for Spanish, press two if you know your extension, press three for company directory, et cetera. Loris shouted, "Operator!" into the phone until finally some overworked call center zombie got on the line and transferred her to the executive offices. From there, a male voice made Loris spell out her name twice and sent her over to a woman with a soothing voice who demanded to know precisely what she wanted to see Mr. Rittenhour about.

"I have in my possession a very rare and unique late-eighteenth-century chief headdress, thought to be from the Austral Islands," Loris said.

The woman put them on hold and in five minutes came back on. "Mr. Rittenhour said that sounds like a museum piece and he does not deal in stolen or misappropriated artifacts," she said in snipped tones.

Loris said she had the paperwork on it, and it was all on the up and up and she'd be happy to explain but only if he were able to come and see it because it wasn't the kind of thing she could transport easily. This statement got Rittenhour to the phone.

"Why aren't you going through a dealer in the proper manner?" he said. Not even a hello.

"I'm working with a client who doesn't want anyone to know he's selling it," Loris said. Zane admired Loris' ability to fabricate stories out of nothing once again. She was a regular artist at it.

"Send me a photo."

"Sure, I can send you all the photos you want. But it won't do it justice. You need to see it in person. I've got other buyers coming tomorrow afternoon to look at it."

"Where is it?"

"It's in Tulsa. A quick flight in the WorthComm jet. Why

don't you come up first thing tomorrow morning and take a look at it?"

Silence on the other end. Zane felt his abs and shoulders tighten. Was the ruse going to work? Then Rittenhour grunted in amusement. "You know what? Sure. I'll come. You have a gallery space or something? Or are we meeting in some dark alley?"

"Meet us at the Port Insurance offices. We have the headdress safe here."

Zane felt a little mortified that they'd just lied to this man to lure him to Tulsa under false pretenses. But Loris said that in-person meetings were the best way to get information and she'd just saved them both a trip to Fort Worth. It would save Kayla the travel expenses. But still, he worried about just what kind of mood Rittenhour would be in once he heard there was no Oceanic headdress, just a bunch of questions about a steakhouse dinner last month in Fort Worth and a dead woman.

Chapter 10
Zane

Thursday morning, the energy was electric in the office. No need for a Ghost redberry drink or any other kind of stimulant this morning. Zane was on edge. He tried to focus on checking the email and social media accounts—what he thought of as "running the traps"—but his focus was scattered, and he looked up like a jackrabbit in the cabbage patch every time someone stepped through the front door.

Then the door swung open, and it was unmistakably Sherwood Rittenhour. Zane recognized him from photos online. Loris spotted him too, raising her hand in greeting and beckoning him back to the office.

"Here we go," she said.

Rittenhour's face was a big ruddy square, his sunburn extending into the opening of his white-and-green striped golf shirt. As he approached, Zane thought he looked his seventy-three years, but he walked like he was fifty-six, quickly and smoothly to the back. Then he stepped into the office and Zane saw his eyes—those looked like he was a hundred and six. Zane watched as the old-looking eyes narrowed, taking in the office, and lingering over the business cards prominently placed on Loris' desk reading "Loris Trapper Investigations."

"Where is it?"

"That was a trick," Loris said. "I don't have an Oceanic headdress. In fact, I've never seen one."

Rittenhour stared at her for a few beats before turning to walk out the door.

"But I have something for you. A message from Dawn Renee," Loris said.

Rittenhour spun back on his heel, his eyes as watchful and ancient as the Komodo dragons at the zoo. "I don't know who that is, and we've already established you're a liar. Why should I care?"

Rittenhour's voice carried out into the main insurance office, where the juice-fast man paused his paperwork and seemed to watch the spectacle unfolding. Words like "you're a liar" often drew people's attention.

"Do you remember running into a woman named Dawn Renee in a steakhouse in Fort Worth last month?" Loris asked.

"What is this?"

"It's personal," Zane said. "You might want some privacy."

Rittenhour didn't look at either of them as he slowly closed the door. "Who are you people?"

"I gave you my real name on the phone. I'm Loris Trapper. I'm a private investigator. This is Zane Clearwater. He works with me. The message isn't actually from Dawn Renee, it's from us. Because she's dead. Someone killed her."

"I'm a fool for coming here but truth be told I was on my way today to play a round at Forest Ridge. So, I'll stand here and let you incriminate yourself so I know exactly what to tell the police when you try to extort money out of me. You've done some research on me but not enough to figure out I don't tolerate blackmailers. But sure, go ahead, give me the pitch."

These weren't the words or actions of a man with a clean conscience, Zane thought. Something compelled him to stay.

"Dawn's daughter, Kayla, is footing the bill and we're committed to her. We're wondering if you know anything about cryptocurrency because Dawn left her daughter a nice share of it," Loris said.

"Cryptocurrency. Keep going."

"Look, Mr. Rittenhour." Zane had an idea for explaining it to him, but when the older man turned those flinty eyes on him, it was harder to speak than he thought. "We didn't have to do it like this. We could have gone the longer road—collecting evidence and interviewing your friends, that kind of thing. But that takes time and money."

"We just want to know what your connection is to Dawn Renee. That way, we can rule you out of our investigation," Loris said.

"There's no connection. This conversation is ridiculous. Do you know how many people I encounter on a daily basis?"

"This was at a steak restaurant called The Bull Farmhouse. Dawn Renee was with another woman who remembers it all, including your strong reaction to hearing she had a daughter."

"I don't know a Dawn Renee," he said. "And I still might fill the police in on this ridiculous conversation. Especially as it seems they are looking for a murderer. It seems like you two are gearing up for some old-fashioned blackmail and you've picked the wrong guy."

The man was stony cold, but he had a tell, Zane thought. Right before he said he didn't know Dawn Renee he did three things: he crossed his arms across his chest, planted his feet as though ready to fight, and flicked his eyes toward the door. He was lying about not knowing Dawn Renee. Zane felt sure of it. He grabbed his phone and held up the graduation day photo of the mother and daughter. Rittenhour glanced at it then set his lips in a firm line with a shake of his head.

"You can call the police," Loris said. "They'll take you seriously, I'm sure, a man of your stature. They'll question us. But we're not blackmailing you, so the inquiry is not going to go anywhere. We're just trying to learn more about your connection with Dawn Renee. So do you still want to call the police?"

Those reptile eyes still hadn't blinked but his sunburn reddened a few shades. "I won't call the police because it's too much trouble to take the time and I have a tee time in—" he checked his watch "—thirty minutes. I know nothing of this Dawn Renee or Kayla, and if this other woman says I do, well, she's mistaken, that's all. Your evidence is flimsy, and I think you have ulterior motives beyond simply uncovering my nonexistent connection to this woman. But I'm glad I met you because it affirms my perception of those who pursue your line of work. Nosy police-wannabes taking advantage of people when they're at their lowest. I have half a mind to call this Kayla and tell her to refuse to pay you. You're incompetent."

He opened the door with a flourish and strode out. It had been a big gamble and it did not pay off. Loris had said it might not, but that extraordinary action could lead to extraordinary things. Something about how you had to push people hard to make them do things quickly. Private investigators didn't have time to sit around and wait for the natural course of events to unfold. They were hired to bring situations to a head with conclusive proof. But had they made a misstep in telling him Kayla's name?

As though Loris was reading his mind, she said, "He could get Kayla's name from the Internet if he wanted. I'm sure it wouldn't take him long to even find out where she lives, whether we told him or not. The question is, if he is the man behind the Bitcoin fortune on Kayla's digital wallet, would our meeting this morning spur him to action? What would it be?"

"I won't forgive myself if anything happens to Kayla," Zane said. He tried to imagine the distinguished, retirement-age, golf-playing telecom billionaire entering Dawn's home with a syringe full of poison, gaining entry into the house, and getting close enough to inject her, then watching her die. The answer was yes, it was conceivable in Zane's mind. Rittenhour was a tough nut and some of the news stories Zane read about him mentioned a reputation for ruthlessness. But it didn't seem likely that Dawn Renee would have let him in the house, not based on the reaction she had to him at the Fort Worth restaurant.

"I'll call Angus and let him know about the Fort Worth meeting. You go tell Kayla about the conversation and tell her I'd like her to go stay with my Uncle Brian and Aunt Tracy for a while. Just until the killer is found. A million dollars could be the motive and Kayla could be the next target."

Zane left the office at Thirty-first and Yale, the whooshing sound of cars in the later stages of morning rush hour on the Broken Arrow Expressway like white noise. He stuck to surface streets for the two-and-a-half-mile drive to Boot Barn at Thirty-first and Memorial. He still remembered the store when it had been locally owned, a western-wear retailer called Drysdale's outfitting Tulsa's suburban cowboys and cowgirls with hats, huge belt buckles, and boots ranging from everyday ropers to fancy alligator-hide. He'd been in there once or twice but not found much in his price range, which was basically zero most of the time. He and Lettie grew up shopping at thrift stores.

He parked in the Boot Barn lot and entered the store. For a weekday morning just after opening, there was a livelier atmosphere than he expected, which was to say two women were watching a video with loud trap music on a phone and laughing in the women's clothing section. To the left, a man restocked a bookshelf with candles with names like "Ponca City" and "Arkansas River." Zane couldn't imagine what smells would greet his nose from those two locations: the rotten egg smell of oil refineries wouldn't sell too many candles. Kayla had a Windex bottle and a cloth and was polishing a long glass case full of shiny belt buckles.

The store was vast with exposed wood beam ceilings that tinged the industrial lighting with a warmer hue. Tables stacked with blue jeans and racks of western-style plaid shirts filled the space behind the glass cases where Kayla was. Tall racks containing cowboy boots of all shapes and sizes extended almost to the ceiling to his left. An upbeat country tune played on the speakers, a woman's voice singing about how she didn't even know her last name because she got so drunk. Zane could relate, at least back in his drinking days.

The establishment smelled of leather and Windex and something vaguely spicy—maybe the Ponca City candle? Zane could see one was burning in the center bullpen where three cash registers sat silent. Near the candles sat a series of photo frames, coffee mugs, and small wooden signs with plucky sayings such as "When you get bucked off, get back on" and "Remember that girl who gave up? Neither does anyone else."

Zane went to Kayla's side. They were a far enough distance from the two women and the man that he felt assured of privacy. He wasn't sure how to deliver the news, so he skipped the finer details but gave her a brief description of Sherwood Rittenhour, the gist of the Fort Worth restaurant encounter,

Rittenhour's reaction, and Loris's suggestion that she stay out in the country with her aunt and uncle.

Kayla burst out laughing, throwing Zane for a loop. Of all the reactions, he didn't see that one coming.

"Zane, you've got to be kidding me, right? Some old rich guy is a suspect in my mother's murder? And you're afraid he's going to come after me? For a million dollars in crypto? He's probably worth *billions*. How did you even get him to talk to you?"

Zane definitely wasn't going to answer that question. It would only earn him a bunch of questions about why they did this and why they didn't say that. Also, he didn't tell Kayla what was next on the program. In the few months he'd worked with Loris, he'd learned that clients would second-guess your moves or make dumb suggestions.

"I really think you ought to consider staying with them. It's nice out in Wagoner County."

Kayla shook her head slightly, her eyes meeting his. "That's like fifty miles away or something. I'm not going to do all that driving to come into work."

"It's thirty miles. Maybe thirty-three. We're just worried about your safety is all."

"I can take care of myself," she said. "My mother taught me how. And you don't need to remind me that my mother was killed. I think about it all the time. Let's just focus on finding that PIN."

Zane gave a speech about the importance of precautions peppered with tempting details of Aunt Tracy's delicious cooking, but he might as well have been trying to convince her that unicorns exist and there was one waiting for her outside. Finally, he extracted a promise from her to let him know immediately if anything unusual or suspicious happened and he considered that as much of a victory as he was going to get.

Kayla had a stubborn streak like his sister and the only way to break it down was to give it time.

He left Boot Barn and, on a whim, headed back out to Delaware Pointe to look at the house where Dawn Renee died. He didn't know how or why, but he had a feeling it would help to see the spot where she died. Even if just from the outside. He parked his car and stood on the side of the road. It was a quiet neighborhood that ended abruptly in vast empty lots stretching into the horizon to the back fences of the home developments to the east. The house where Dawn had lived was large and stately, with a high-pitched roof and grey stone walls accented with wood siding. An oak tree shimmered with new green leaves in the front yard, and bright pink flowers dotted the azalea bushes planted along the walkway. No one stirred behind the windows. Someone, maybe Kayla, had staked a small white wooden cross in the ground near the driveway. Small enough and dusty enough that Zane hadn't noticed it at first. He cleaned it off with the edge of his jacket, so it shone white again.

Everything looked so perfect and prosperous in this neighborhood, but someone was murdered in this house. Death sprang up everywhere, a relentless whack-a-mole game with grim consequences. Good neighborhoods or bad ones, tragedies happened all the time. The realization, coupled with the beauty of the spring morning, made Zane feel sad even as he admired the golden sun sparkling through low, thin strands of clouds smeared across a robin's egg-blue sky.

Light only exists because of darkness.

Old Spice had said the video camera footage captured from the neighbors only showed a lone figure walking up to the door. Surely a car on the street would get a little bit of attention in this quiet neighborhood. He contemplated coming back to ask around when more people were home in the evening. Though surely the police would have done that already. The idea of the police arresting Sherwood Rittenhour came into his mind, and he relished the idea of the flinty-eyed old man in handcuffs. But he had to be careful not to jump to conclusions. After all, how things look wasn't always how things were.

Chapter 11
Zane

Zane's phone rang as he pulled into an open parking spot in front of Tiffany's apartment building on Thursday evening. Tiffany's beautiful face popped up on FaceTime. He smiled to hide the sinking feeling that she was calling once again to cancel on him. It was happening so often these days as Cell Phone Fix-It consumed her every waking moment.

"Hey baby," he said.

"Hey, handsome. I was just calling to say I was going to be late. Are you already there?"

"Yeah, but I can wait. How long do you think you'll be?"

He listened to her wind her way through the problems of the day before she estimated another thirty minutes at the store.

"But you can go up. Kayla's there. Get a soda, relax. I'll be home soon." She gazed absentmindedly at the phone, not seeming to really see him. She started chewing her lip like it had been dipped in sugar, a sure sign she was worried about something.

He took a deep breath to try to shake off his disappointment at having to wait to see her. "Go easy on that lip. If anyone is going to bite it, I want it to be me," he said.

She gave him a weak smile.

"You look worried. I'll let you get finished and you can tell me all about it when you get home, okay? Just hurry."

She looked grateful and they hung up with a couple of "I love you's" thrown in for reassurance.

Kayla answered the door right away, telling him how glad she was to see him. She looked younger than Lettie in a red sweatshirt decorated with two flowers and the question "What if all it works out?" on the front. She wore very little makeup, and her hair was combed back and anchored behind her ears.

"Do you have news?" she said.

Zane shook his head. "Sorry to disappoint you but I'm here to meet Tiffany. She's running a little late but asked me to come up."

Kayla lowered her head and stared at the carpet as though it had turned into a field of flowers as she stepped back to let him into the apartment. "Do you know how long these things take?"

"It depends," Zane said. "Anywhere between a couple of months and a year."

She nodded. "Right. But what about you and Loris finding the PIN? How long do you expect that to take?"

Her question startled him, but he tried not to show it. "I told you at the start, it takes a while. We knock on a lot of doors and run up and down a lot of dead ends sometimes. I can give you a full report if you want it in writing."

"It's just that... I don't mean to sound like I don't care about my mom, but are you following the news about this latest crypto scandal? All the prices are falling. I've probably lost thousands of dollars over the past two days."

"You've still got a decent chunk of change in that hard wallet," Zane said.

"But it's lessening daily." She pressed her lips together. "I want to ask you something about this man you met. Do you think there's any chance he's related to her? Or that he's my father?"

"What makes you think that?"

Kayla crossed to the kitchen counter to pick up a half-full bottle of beer and took a long swig. From the way she wobbled as she walked, he guessed it wasn't her first drink of the evening. "I'm going to tell you something she told me once. A long time ago. I've never told anyone."

A tingle started up around the base of Zane's spine. He felt the urge to grab his phone and record her, an old instinct from police training days. Breakthroughs came in all different ways.

"I told you my father was a sperm donor, didn't I? My mom went to a place and just picked out some rando guy to make a baby with. Like she was shopping for a handbag." A cavalcade of emotions passed through Kayla's face as she spoke: embarrassment morphing to disgust to anger. She swallowed them all down with a gulp of beer.

"When did you find out?"

"For years she told me my dad was out of the picture because he was someone she didn't know well. I think I was thirteen or something when she specifically told me about the sperm bank. Some family heritage project at school. She told me the news like she was telling me she forgot to pack my lunch. Like I said, Mom wasn't a warm and fuzzy person." She brushed the backside of her hand under her nose like a small child with a cold. Tears lurked behind her twisted smile.

"That's rough."

"But what if that wasn't the truth? What if she just didn't want me to know who my father was?"

"Couldn't you take one of those DNA tests? See if that unlocks any connections?"

"I've thought about it." Kayla rubbed the back of her neck without looking at Zane. "You see what I'm saying though, right? My mom was big on privacy. She didn't want me to know her. I don't think she even liked me that much. I don't know why she bothered to have me." She snorted then took another swig of beer.

"I was at your mom's house today," Zane said. "Someone put a white cross in the front yard, near the curb."

Kayla played with the corner of the label on her beer. "That was me. I took that little cross from a floral arrangement someone sent last week. Mom wasn't Christian or anything, well, not such that she went to church. It's still there?"

"It's still there."

"Hmm, that's nice. I thought maybe the landscaper, or someone would have trashed it by now."

"People surprise me all the time with their goodness," Zane said.

"You're a smart man, Zane Clearwater. Shall we sit down?" She wobbled to the couch and plopped onto a cushion, her body shaped like the letter "C" against the cushions. Zane took a seat at the opposite end. "Oh, silly me! Do you want something to drink?" She held out a hand, lurching forward as though she meant to struggle back to her feet.

"No, no I'm good," he said. "Stay where you are."

"It's funny what you say about people surprising you with their goodness. I had an encounter like that today."

Zane drew a deep breath through the nose, grateful for the change in topic. "What happened today?"

"Have you ever heard how Kate Upton was discovered somewhere random, like a horse show?"

"Is Kate Upton a model or something?"

With an arched eyebrow and a deadpan tone, she retorted, "I guess Tiffany's been hiding those Sports Illustrated swimsuit issues from you, huh? Yeah, anyway, that is what happened to me today, if you can believe it. I mean, not to be in a movie or anything like that, but there I was, working my shift at Boot Barn, helping some old man pick out ostrich boots and we get to talking and I tell him about how I'm trying to get a job as a physical therapist. Turns out he's some tech entrepreneur starting an online health clinic for men to get things like medicine for hair growth or you know, sex problems," she said, blushing prettily. "He said they were looking for someone to be the face for their videos and social media and that with my background in medicine, I'd be a good fit."

"That's kind of weird," Zane said. "So, he offered you a job on the spot?"

"He said he'd have to run it by his partners and I might have to do an audition video or something, or maybe meet with them. They are in Plano, Texas, so maybe a video call."

The encounter sounded entirely sketchy to Zane, and he couldn't believe she was considering it. "What was he doing in Tulsa? Is he from Plano?" If Zane was remembering his Texas geography correctly, Plano was about an hour northeast of Fort Worth, so the location sharpened his attention.

"I think he said he had family here in Tulsa he was visiting," she said, either unaware or unfazed by the connection. She stood up and wove her way back to the kitchen counter, grabbed something, and came back to hand Zane a business card. It read "Tyler Swinton, President and CEO, Valor Medicine for Men" and had an address in Plano.

"I just told you I thought you ought to take some precautions, given your mother's murder and that Bitcoin wallet. Don't you see that this seems... strange?"

She shrugged. "I don't know. Maybe its unrelated. And he

said I could work remote. Ever since the pandemic, he said, they were set up to work virtually so it was no problem."

"Did you tell him where you live?"

"I'm not an idiot." Kayla rocked back and forth on her heels for a moment before falling onto the sofa next to Zane. Her head bobbed a bit as she wavered on the seat. Instinctively he reached out to steady her, and she grabbed his thigh to stop herself from sliding on the floor.

"Nice quads," she said, squeezing his thigh right above the knee and making him jump.

"Time for bed, I think," he said. "No more beers for you."

"You're very handsome, you know that, right?"

He maneuvered Kayla into her bedroom, luring her with the promise of a fresh beer he never had to deliver on because she had passed out by the time he returned. Good. And all just in time, as keys jangled in the hallway and the lock clicked open. The door swung inward as Tiffany entered the apartment, her warm smile spreading when she saw him.

Disaster averted, or so Zane thought.

He and Tiffany woke up the next morning in each other's arms in a love-drunk hangover, but Kayla spoiled the mood in the kitchen pretty fast. Zane was spearing one of those coffee pods into Tiffany's Keurig knock-off coffeemaker when Kayla staggered out of her bedroom to look for an aspirin. Upon seeing Zane and Tiffany, she decided she had to apologize. Sorry she drank so much, sorry she might have come on a little strong, on and on. Tiffany's smile took on a pained look that didn't seem to register with Kayla.

Of course, Tiffany didn't make a fuss about this out-of-the blue apology. It wasn't her style, or at least not while she was trying to figure out the score. But as far as she knew, Kayla had only seen Zane a few times and at the most for the thirty minutes last night, so she had to be wondering just what had happened in the apartment before she came home. Zane couldn't tell her that Kayla had hired him and Loris to help her access a million dollars in Bitcoin, so he kept his mouth shut. He and Tiffany had built up a lot of trust over the year they had been together, so he'd have to lean on that goodwill until the case was over or Kayla freed him from the confidentiality. But the question hung in the air as they said goodbye.

Fifteen minutes later, he was almost at Loris's office when his phone rang, and the cartoon avatar Tiffany used for her profile picture filled his phone screen. He barely got the word "hello" out before she snapped at him.

"Now why on earth would you be in my roommate's favorite contacts on her phone?"

"What?" Zane asked immediately.

He made no response as she admitted that her suspicions lead her to snoop on Kayla's phone. Not only had Zane made the favorites list but there were also a handful of calls between them. Tiffany's voice was stormy and suffering. He could hear the car's turn signal clicking and worried about her driving when she was so emotional and distracted.

"Let me come see you. Are you on the way to the store?"

"Yes." Her tone was clipped.

"Just concentrate on driving. I'll be there in ten minutes. I'll explain. There's nothing for you to worry about," Zane said. "I love you."

Silence.

"I'm coming over there, okay?"

More silence.

"Are you there?" he asked.

"Yes, okay," Tiffany said finally, as though trying to regain her composure. "I'll see you then."

As Zane drove back across town, a light rain dropped onto the car and the road before him. The sky was grey and low. He tried to think of how to tell Tiffany that Kayla was a client without telling her Kayla was a client but didn't come up with any good ideas. He dialed Kayla who croaked a hello into the phone.

"Tiffany's not happy with me," he said. "She thinks there's something between us."

"I thought that might be the case. She frosted me out when she left this morning."

"I need to tell her you are my client. Do I have your permission?"

"How much are you going to tell her?"

"The bare minimum. But I need to do something, Kayla. I love her. I can't let this come between us."

"Um, okay. I guess I brought this problem on," she said in a tiny voice. "I just don't want her to think—oh, I don't know what I want her to think. It's fine."

The Cell Phone Fix-It store on Eleventh Street was in a small two-story building attached to another building that also housed a thrift shop and an auto parts store. He parked in back by the large metal bins next to Tiffany's car, the engine still giving off warmth, and entered through the back door. Tiffany had her back to him and was talking to her employee, Ricky, about some problem with the credit card machine. The store was bright and pleasing in its order—shelves of phone cases, screen protectors, chargers, cords, earbuds and headsets, disposable phones—like a reflection of Tiffany's optimism and usually sunny personality. The unpleasantness of their call receded a bit in the cheery store as he watched her patiently show Ricky how to reset the wireless credit card reader. There was no sign of impatience on her face. And when she saw Zane standing in the back, she even gave him a small, rueful smile.

"Hey, Zane!" Ricky called out. He had round cheeks and small eyes that peeped through enormous, black-framed glasses. His shoulders sloped forward, as though he was apologizing for something. "I was just telling Tiffany I'm sorry I don't have the hang of this credit card machine yet. I know she wants to spend less time here not more."

"You've only been working here two weeks, Ricky," Tiffany said. "No big deal."

Zane listened with half an ear as they talked about hard resets and where the Wi-Fi router was as he tried to compose his thoughts. How much of her life had Kayla shared with Tiffany? What about the cryptocurrency? He wrestled with the amount of information to give his girlfriend. Tiffany was so important to him. He couldn't stand for her to be stewing in jealousy or uncertainty—his love for her was complete. But Kayla had told him about her past in confidence.

"Let's talk in the office," Tiffany said when she had finished with Ricky. She waved him into the narrow storage space in the back where a desk and computer shared space with boxes of inventory and holiday decorations.

"I know you're mad and you have some questions," Zane said. He wanted to put his arms around her, but she had a bristly energy around her like a protective cloak.

"Yes and no," she said, her face turned to him with wary interest. "After I hung up with you, I realized... her mother was murdered. She's probably asking for your help with that."

"You get that I can't say anything, right? People come to us in confidence and—"

"I feel so stupid. But why doesn't she trust me enough to tell me this? You see why this would make me upset, right?"

"I do. I get it. And I don't know why she wouldn't tell you. Some people are very private. I think it was how she was raised."

"But that's it, then? You're helping her with something related to her mother's death?"

"Yes," said Zane simply. A small motion of dissatisfaction seemed to pass over Tiffany's face, but it vanished when he stepped toward her for a hug.

"Do you want to go get a quick cup of coffee?" he asked.

"No, I need to do some stuff," she said, gesturing with one slim hand at the computer. Was her refusal a remnant of her irritation with him over this secrecy with Kayla or her business-owner's drive to work long hours? He tried to put the question out of his mind.

Chapter 12
Zane

Back at the office on Friday morning, Zane searched the web for Tyler Swinton's name, finding his photo easily on the Valor Medicine for Men webpage. He scanned his biography which listed a bunch of companies Zane had never heard of. There were two exceptions. Swinton had worked at the energy company Enron right up until its massive financial scandal and bankruptcy in 2001. After that, he worked in business development at none other than —WorthComm.

His internal danger radar started flashing red. He didn't like the coincidence. WorthComm could hold the key to this mystery. He needed to find some people who worked for the firm back in the early 2000s before Dawn showed up at Pickert's office with a baby and see if he could find some connections.

Zane channeled Lettie as he tried to do some online sleuthing on LinkedIn. It operated like a Facebook for professional people: a place to post résumés and career news. Loris paid for a feature called Sales Navigator that allowed you to search all the names and profiles of employees of a company, so he started by looking for people who worked for WorthComm. That search returned eighty-nine thousand people. Way too many to sift through. He opened the advanced search filter, checking boxes to search only those working at the Fort Worth office, in information technology, with twenty-plus years of experience, and who had worked there in the past. This cut the list to about eight-and-a-half thousand. Still too many to sort. He'd have to try a different tactic.

Starting at the top of the long list, he clicked through to read the bios. When he found one that indicated the person had worked at WorthComm around the early 2000s, he saved it into a leads list. He had to click through about a hundred profiles until he'd collected five names of people who worked in IT at WorthComm in the year before Dawn answered Terry Pickert's ad. He shot off LinkedIn InMail messages to the list of five along with the photo of Dawn Renee, not hopeful that the exercise would yield results. He marked his place so he could come back to the longer list of eight-and-a-half thousand if he ran out of other ideas.

Then another idea occurred to him. Back to the LinkedIn home page, he searched for WorthComm alumni and came up with three networking groups for former and current employees of the telecom giant. WorthComm Alumni had five thousand members, WorthComm Alumni Network had one thousand, and WorthComm Fort Worth Alumni had 281 members. He clicked the "Join" button on all three and got back the same message for each: "Your request to join has been sent to the group administrators." Fine. A lot of detective work was waiting for people to get back to you. He didn't hold out a lot of hope they'd approve the request anyway.

On to Reddit. The self-described "front page of the Internet," Reddit operated like a vast message board on every topic under the sun. The site was organized by "subreddits," each of which covered a different topic. Subreddits existed on politics, football, television shows, video games, and weird or specific ones such as "r/FormerPizzaHuts" and "r/BreadStapledto-Trees." He resisted the temptation to check in on "r/Birds-WithArms" and did another search for WorthComm to see what popped up. On this site, he only found one "r/Worth-Comm" and it seemed to mainly focus on the consumer experience of using their new gaming microchip. He typed out a message to leave in the community along with Dawn's photograph, asking if anyone knew her as someone who worked at WorthComm in the early 2000s but omitting her name.

Next up, he went into "r/UnresolvedMysteries," a huge subreddit with nearly two million members, dedicated to unsolved crimes. This community was full of growing numbers of amateur Internet sleuths who posted news stories and cases to gather analysis and speculation from the hive mind of the Internet. Here, he spent more time crafting his post, outlining the circumstances of the murder, describing Dawn Renee's work at Pickert Real Estate, and mentioning that she had some connections to WorthComm from years ago.

He kept at it until Loris returned to the office an hour later.

"Let me show you something," Zane said before she had a chance to put her bag and keys down.

"I've been mining this subreddit on WorthComm for information, and there's this user named QuarterSubstantial who seems to have an axe to grind with the company going back twenty years. They come at Rittenhour pretty hard for what they say was his fundamental mistake to provide the processor for the iPhone. QuarterSubstantial says Rittenhour misjudged the sales potential of the iPhone, turning down the chance to provide the processors because Apple would never sell enough iPhones."

"They got that wrong," Loris said, holding up hers. It seemed like everyone had an iPhone these days. Even Zane had managed to find one he could afford: refurbished and five years old.

"Yeah. Their point is that the company still isn't a significant player in the mobile device market, and they could have been. Rittenhour thought the future was personal computers, not smartphones. And when WorthComm had to lay-off five thousand people a few years back, QuarterSubstantial saw that as directly because of that decision."

"Okay, but so what? WorthComm may have misstepped but it's still a billion-dollar company."

"Maybe I've been in the weeds too long on this subreddit. But I want to reach out to QuarterSubstantial. In another post, they mention that they worked at WorthComm back during that time period and honestly, they just seem like they want to spill the beans."

"Do it. You don't need my permission," Loris said.

Zane knew he didn't need her permission. After all, he'd been sending messages all day trying to root out someone who worked at WorthComm during the period in question. But it was nice not to work in isolation after a morning of staring at screens and typing on keyboards. However, Loris seemed distracted.

He composed a quick message to QuarterSubstantial:

Hey, I'm a private investigator trying to see if there are any connections between WorthComm back in the early two-thousands and a woman who was killed in Tulsa recently. The family thinks there might be. I'd love to pick your brain for a few moments.

Three dots appeared in the Reddit message app, indicating that QuarterSubstantial was typing a reply.

Sure. Are you in Tulsa?

Zane typed back a yes.

I'm in Claremore. Want to meet IRL?

Amazing luck. Maybe he should buy a lottery ticket. Meeting randos off the Internet wasn't something Zane would normally recommend, but he'd read enough of QuarterSubstantial's posts to have a feel for the person as cranky but not likely to be violent or dangerous. Besides, Loris was always saying the best way to get information from people was the old-fashioned way: in person. There was nothing more revealing than being able to hear their words and match them with body language, tone, and facial expressions. Email and text messages would never replace that. Even video calls didn't give the full picture.

Sure, let's do it.

A few hours later, Zane was parked outside a sports bar in east Tulsa, a squat cinderblock building that had the unappealing name of NO PLACE emblazoned on a cheap blue vinyl banner over the door. The bar clearly had an identity crisis. The banner also presented four different types of entertainment: cocktails, karaoke, pool, and golf simulators. He'd gotten used to sitting in bars even though he no longer drank alcohol, but that didn't mean he wasn't tempted all the time.

He stared for a moment out the windshield, trying to collect his thoughts. QuarterSubstantial had been downright excited to talk about WorthComm. His name was Derek, and Zane expected to see a guy in his fifties, bitter and gossipy.

The bar wasn't all that crowded on a Friday afternoon, but it was fairly noisy, with classic rock blasting in the background, songs by Billy Squier and Queen and Tom Petty. The current selection of "Lonely is the Night" had inspired one guy at the bar to play air guitar. These songs were before Zane's time, but he still knew the lyrics as well as any aging Boomer in the room because they played constantly on the

Tulsa radio station his mother had favored when he was growing up.

No more lazing round the TV, you'll go crazy, come out with me.

This Billy Squier song which had been one of his mother's favorites was still playing when Zane saw a woman waving at him from a table by the bar. She was in her mid-fifties, petite and soft-bodied, with fuzzy, grey hair pulled back in a fat braid that extended halfway down her back. Bright blue reading glasses perched on the end of her nose. Two cell phones sat in front of her on the table next to a half-full glass of beer. She wore an enormous wristwatch that looked like it would keep time on the ocean floor.

"Derek?" he said, trying not to let his confusion show on his face. He shouldn't have made any pre-judgments about what kind of person to expect. But after chatting with QuarterSubstantial online, Zane had formed a mental picture of a disgruntled man in his fifties, a pale, unshaven mess, the kind of guy who spent all his time drinking energy drinks and staring into the light of his computer monitors. Perhaps wearing T-shirts with slogans like "One Nation, Under Surveillance" or "Privacy is Dead." With her peasant-style floral blouse, long crinkly skirt, and lace-up boots, this woman was dressed like she could be working at Earth Spells, the occult store Lettie used to go to.

"Derrick but ending in -ick," she said. "Like the oil derrick. My dad was a roustabout on an oil rig, and I guess he just couldn't get enough of it. Nice to meet you."

"But online you said it was Derek, with an ek at the end."

"That's my male online persona. Makes things easier out there on the interwebs to be a man."

Zane wasn't sure that the name Derrick with an -ick was necessarily a feminine name but he kept the thought to himself. He ordered a Coca-Cola from the big-eared bartender and slid into the seat opposite Derrick. They did the polite chit-chat thing for a bit, talking about the cool weather and how Elton John had come to play the BoK Center and the spring crop of thunderstorms and tornados until the bartender delivered Zane's soft drink. Zane waved off the offer of a plastic straw because Lettie had told him single-use plastics like that were killing the sea turtles or something and took a sip.

Derrick said she only had an hour or so to talk and asked what Zane wanted to know about WorthComm in the early two-thousands. Zane filled her in on the basics and said they were trying to find someone who could identify a woman who may have worked there back then. He grabbed his phone, flicked to the photo, and handed it to Derrick.

She squinted for a beat, then flicked at the screen to make Dawn's face bigger for a moment before returning it to regular size. She looked at Zane.

"Why," she said, "that's Diana Granger. Older now, but aren't we all? But yes, I'm sure."

Zane tried not to look surprised. "Good," he said. "At least we have her name. Did you work with her?" But he realized he'd forgotten how much he had shared online; he'd posted on Reddit that they were looking into the death of Dawn Renee. So, he continued, "The name we have for her is Dawn Renee. That photo was taken a few months before she died."

"She died? That's terrible," Derrick was frowning. "Why did she change her name?" She gripped Zane's phone and enlarged the photo on the screen again. "Was she involved in some sort of crime?"

"It's a long story," Zane said. "And some of it is confidential to my client, but there is a hard wallet with about a million dollars of cryptocurrency on it and we're not sure how Dawn got it. We're just running down different angles and it seems like there's a connection to WorthComm. I don't think you'd pass anything on to anyone there."

"I'm not a big fan as you can tell." Derrick handed back Zane's phone.

"Definitely, but you know how it is. Better to be careful these days. Information spreads so fast. But you may have figured out that the folks at WorthComm might not want what we're working on to come out. Particularly Sherwood Rittenhour. So, I'd be grateful if you told me about Diana Granger. Did Rittenhour know her?"

She nodded. "Definitely. She was hired to help him research and write his autobiography. I met her at one of the holiday parties at his home. She was young, fresh out of college, into computer science, and looking to get her start. Somehow, she landed this research assistant gig with one of the most powerful men in telecom. She was very intelligent and competent."

The conversation lasted more than an hour, but Derrick didn't seem in any mad rush to leave. Zane filled several notebook pages with the following facts about Diana Granger, all according to Derrick.

She had first seen Diana at the Rittenhour mansion in Westover Hills when Diana had started as Rittenhour's autobiography research assistant in June 1999. At that time, Rittenhour was riding high, the stock price for WorthComm approaching its 2000 bubble high of $350 per share. Stock market analysts were predicting it would hit $1,000 a share. It never did. The price topped out at $400 and then plummeted. Over three weeks the stock price had dropped to $175 and was seen by many as the beginning of the end of that dot-com bubble. The book deal eventually got scrapped, but Rittenhour found Diana a job in the business development department sometime around January 2001.

As for her background, Derrick remembered that Diana had come from some small town outside Arlington, and that she'd graduated from Southern Methodist University. But she didn't know much else, like if she had family still in Arlington or any personal connections to Rittenhour other than the job.

It was a good start, Zane thought, a fruitful beginning to the origins of Dawn Renee and definite evidence tying her to Rittenhour. The man had been lying when he said he didn't recognize her. But Derrick didn't have much to offer when it came to what happened to Dawn aka Diana around 2001. She suddenly wasn't there any longer. The last time Derrick saw her was probably March or April 2001, but she didn't remember hearing about her leaving or why and she hadn't really thought much of it.

Derrick also didn't know much about Diana's relationships with others. She had liked her and admired her work ethic, but Derrick had been consumed with the care of her autistic son back then, so her attention was not on making work friends. She remembered that she'd had the idea that Diana had been friendly with Rittenhour's son, Curtis, who had been in his mid-thirties back then, but she didn't recall anything specific to point to. The big question was whether it seemed like Diana/Dawn had been intimate with Rittenhour. On this, Zane could tell that Derrick really wanted to deliver the goods but that she couldn't remember anything specific, and she was too honest to make something up. The two were alone together a lot, but when Derrick tried to remember any incident that pointed to it being more than a work relationship, nothing came to her.

Zane filled four pages of notes before Derrick excused herself. Zane remained at the table for a few moments, finishing his Coke and writing out a timeline of Diana/Dawn's life that looked something like this:

Diana Granger Timeline
From Derrick "QuarterSubstantial"

Up to 1995
Not known, but probably outside of Arlington, Texas

1995 to 1999
Probably a student at Southern Methodist University

June 1999
Hired by Sherwood Rittenhour as autobiography research assistant

January 2001
Gets a job in WorthComm business development department

March 2001
Kayla Renee conceived

April 2001
Diana Granger seems to drop off the face of the earth

December 4, 2001
Kayla Renee's birthday

August 14, 2002
Dawn Renee applies for job at Pickert Real Estate in Tulsa

Last month
Dawn Renee runs into Sherwood Rittenhour at Fort Worth steakhouse, according to Martina Decomo

It wasn't much, but Dawn Renee's life was slowly coming into focus.

Chapter 13
Zane

"What do you know about Dawn Renee's boyfriend, Gabriel?"

"No hello, how are you? Who is this anyway?" Zane leaned back in his chair and lowered the volume on his earbuds so Old Spice's voice wasn't playing at top decibels like the country music he had just been listening to.

"I'm calling about your car warranty. It's expired. Just tell me what you know about this Gabriel"—Old Spice paused a moment as though consulting his notes—"Gabriel Connor."

"Just what you told us. I went to go talk to him, but he wasn't cooperative. He didn't tell me anything."

"He's dead."

Gabriel's last words to Zane stuck in his mind. That barking laugh and his offhand "Good luck with that" as he closed the door in Zane's face. Zane had had a feeling the man knew more than he was willing to share. And now he was dead.

Old Spice continued: "Could be a carjacking gone wrong. That's what it looks like anyway. He was shot. Texts between him and Dawn going back a few months show they were still in regular contact even though he said they had broken up. You don't know anything?"

"I don't know anything more than I told you. Do you think Kayla's in danger?" Zane went on to tell him about Swinton and Kayla's refusal to move out to Uncle Brian and Aunt Tracy's house.

"We could assign police protection to her," Old Spice said. "But if she had a place like that to go where no one might think to look for her, that would be a good idea. Just until we get it sorted."

It was just after four o'clock on Monday when Zane pulled into the Boot Barn parking lot. The place looked deserted. Gigantic posters of Lucchese boots and Wrangler jeans hung on either side of a massive red barn façade partially covering the rectangular box building. The store had two wooden barn doors flanking the automatic sliding glass doors. Zane resisted the urge to tug on one of the barn doors to see what would happen. Inside, a vacuum cleaner whirred from somewhere in the back, and country music twanged from the loudspeakers. The air seemed stuffy, scented with leather.

He texted Kayla he was here, and she texted right back that she was in the boot section and could he meet her. He found her in the third aisle from the door, surrounded by five-foot-tall wooden shelves stacked with a dazzling array of cowboy boots. Sharply pointed toes to soft rounded ones to square-toed shit-kickers in every shade of brown and black imaginable with some reds and blues thrown in. Some were plain and others featured gorgeous embroidery and leather work decorating the boot shafts and vamps. Cowhide, ostrich, goat, snake, and lizard leathers added to the visual feast, but Kayla seemed oblivious to the beauty around her. She smiled nervously when she saw him. She looked drawn, dark circles like bruises under her eyes. She took a drink from a tall metal bottle of water and her hand was shaking slightly.

"Hi Zane, what's going on that you needed to talk in person?"

Zane took a seat on one of the padded wooden shoe benches affixed with mirrors so customers could admire the look of the shoes on their feet. "A couple of things. First, I wanted to tell you that we believe your mother's name used to be Diana Granger and that she worked at WorthComm back before you were born. Have you ever heard her use that name or talk about WorthComm?"

She paused, deep in thought, as if she was accessing information from her mental database. "I don't think so. Why did she change her name?"

"We haven't figured that out yet. We're working on it. Have you had any more contact with Tyler Swinton?"

"No, not yet. Why?"

"Today there was a development. I don't want to scare you blind, but your mother's boyfriend, Gabriel Connor, was found dead. Shot."

Her eyes widened. "Where? How?"

"I don't know anything other than that it looks like a carjacking, but you never know. It could be a case of wrong place, wrong time; or it could be related to your mom's death. But we want to keep you safe just in case."

"You're scaring me, Zane. I know you said you didn't want to do that, but you are. Her name change, this WorthComm connection, and what does this all have to do with Tyler Swinton?"

"I'm not sure there's a connection but there are a few coincidences that have me nervous. The way he just showed up in your life and offered you a job. Maybe it's nothing. But the bottom line is that your mother was killed and then her boyfriend and I'd like to have you leave here now. We can give some excuse about an urgent family matter. I want to take you out to Loris's uncle and aunt's house to stay. Are you sure you didn't tell this Tyler Swinton where you lived?"

She squinted and frowned at him. "No, not specifically. I might have mentioned I lived around here in an apartment, but I didn't say the street name or anything."

"What about filling out any kind of application for that job with him? Did you give him a résumé, fill out any kind of form?"

"No, but I did help him find my Instagram account. Now you're really scaring me." She pulled a full quill ostrich boot into her lap and started rubbing the soft bumps on the leather like a worry stone.

"Uncle Brian and Aunt Tracy Trapper will take good care of you. And you'll like them. I promise."

"But my manager is going to kill me if I leave my shift now. I'm supposed to work another six hours."

"I don't think we should be messing around here. If you want, I'll talk to your manager. I just want to get you safe and away from where someone can find you if they wanted to. Just until we know more."

"But you can't expect me to just—"

"I'm sorry to cut you off, Kayla, but I think this is important. Now either you're going to talk to your manager, or I am, then we're leaving here to collect a few things from your apartment, and I'm driving you out to the Trappers'."

To Kayla's credit, she handled the talk with the manager and packing up with efficiency and a stoicism Zane hadn't expected. He dropped her off at the Trappers' farmhouse, set in the middle of two hundred acres of flatlands and shielded from the road by tall trees, feeling assured of her safety there. Uncle Brian's collection of rifles added an extra layer of protection. If the couple had any questions about who Kayla was or why she needed to stay there, Loris must have answered them because Uncle Brian and Aunt Tracy welcomed her like a long-lost cousin. Zane declined the offer of lunch despite the delicious smell of catfish emanating from the kitchen and got back on the road.

Zane had told Tiffany he would be at the store by seven, and it was five minutes short of that when he walked through the door. She was alone, leaning on the glass-top counter drinking from a tall to-go paper coffee cup. Letters and numbers were scrawled across the cup, telling Zane that his girlfriend was drinking one of her complicated drinks. Last time he had gotten coffee with her it had been a non-fat Frappuccino with extra whipped cream and chocolate sauce. Just seeing her produced a low and pleasant hum that warmed him from head to toe.

He crossed the tile floor to step behind the counter and clasped her to him. "Hey sweetie," he said, skimming his lips along the sweep of her cheek. Normally she would melt into him but today he could feel her stiffen a bit.

Was Tiffany still annoyed about Kayla? Possibly. Best to get right to it then.

He broke away from the embrace. "I'll skip the chit-chat because I'm working and so are you."

"Okay," she said with eyebrows raised.

"It's about Kayla's case. There have been some developments and it's possible that Kayla herself may be a target. We've got her staying at a safe place out in Wagoner County, and I'd like to stay in the apartment with you just in case."

"That sounds ominous, but you don't need any special invitation to come sleep in my bed," Tiffany said. "Open invitation."

"I think it's just for a couple of days. It could be a couple of weeks. I'm not sure."

"Of course."

Zane glanced at his phone: two new texts from Loris. He needed to return to the office, but the allure of staying by Tiffany's side was hard to resist.

"I wish I could stay, Tiff, you know I do," Zane sighed, his fingers brushing against hers, "but duty calls, and I need to head back to the office. I promise I'll be back as soon as I can."

Chapter 14
Zane

"We're going to have to go to Fort Worth," Loris said around lunchtime on Monday. "I don't think we can get Rittenhour to come to us again, and we need to see him face-to-face."

She held a printed copy of the Diana Granger timeline in front of her. "Did you run a background check with the new name?"

Zane nodded. "Didn't get much other than the SMU registrar confirming she was a student there from 1995 to 1999 and that she earned a computer science degree with honors. Still no hits on where she lived before college. She really does vanish right around spring 2001."

"Good work," Loris said.

Zane pulled out his phone. "Let me just call Tiffany and ask her to stay with her dad and stepmom while I'm gone. Just in case."

The drive to Fort Worth was four-and-a-half hours of four-lane freeways through country vistas. Vast fields stretched for miles, punctuated every thirty miles or so with gas stations and fast-food signs. The afternoon turned into evening, the sky fading to a bruised blue as Loris pulled in for a pitstop at the busy Buc-ees travel center in a Texas town called Melissa just short of Fort Worth. Loris found a spot at an open fuel dispenser, one of dozens and dozens in a maze of gas pumps, while Zane went to the restrooms to see if they lived up to the billing of "cleanest restrooms in America" on the sign. He was pleased to find nothing to complain about. Pretty good for a truck stop. He grabbed two chopped barbecue brisket sandwiches, some energy drinks, and water, and took a selfie with the metal statue of the cartoon beaver that was the store's mascot. Road trips were fun, especially when the destination included the chance to tell a rich jerk that you were on to his lies. Zane couldn't wait to get there and see the look on his face when they presented him with the evidence. He must have recognized Diana/Dawn when they showed him her photo, so he had to expect they were going to get the rest of the story soon enough.

Back in the car, Zane asked Loris why she thought he hadn't just confessed then and there.

"Men like that have been told for most of their lives they are smarter than everyone around them. He figured he would outsmart us." Loris took a bite of the brisket sandwich as she merged back onto the highway. "I love this next part though. Nothing better than being underestimated, right?"

It was dark enough for midnight at seven-thirty that evening when Loris turned the Suburban onto the long driveway leading to the Rittenhour mansion in Westover Hills. Storm clouds hid the moon and stars, and thunder began to rumble followed by flashes of lightning as she put the car into park. Zane pulled the hood of his rain jacket over his head and opened the door. He and Loris dashed across the sidewalk to the covered doorstep for shelter.

"Who is this?" The woman's voice—thick, with a Southern accent—came out scratchy over the video doorbell speaker.

"Loris Trapper and Zane Clearwater," Loris said, leaning toward the camera lens above the speaker. "Mr. Rittenhour knows who we are."

A long pause, then the sound of footsteps behind the door. A tiny woman appeared. She wore a denim work shirt embroidered with ladybugs and butterflies, but all Zane could look at was her right eye, which appeared to have two pupils instead of one. Was this what people meant by the evil eye? He tore his gaze away and forced himself to observe her other features: she was short, middle-aged, with red, chapped hands.

"He's expecting you?" She inspected Zane and Loris from head to toe.

"He is expecting us," Loris said.

The woman squinted her three eyes at them, skeptical. "I'll just ask him then."

She shut the door, leaving them huddled on the porch barely shielded from the rain blown sideways by the strong wind. A few minutes passed then her voice rang out from the doorbell speaker once again. "He will not see you. He says you should leave his property now and if you don't, I'm to call the police. He is a very big supporter of local law—"

"Yeah. Excuse me for interrupting, but I thought he'd say that. Tell him we want to ask him some questions about Diana Granger. He'll recognize that name. We'll wait."

"You're a persistent one, aren't you? You better not be giving me the run-around here."

"He'll see us," Zane said. "He won't like it, but he'll see us. Please just pass on the message."

A few more beats of silence, then the woman said, "Okay."

This time the wait was very long. They heard the footsteps again and the door swung open. The woman, now holding a mobile phone in one hand, stepped to the side to allow them entrance into the foyer and pointed them into a room lined with bookshelves to the right. With a final look of disapproval, she disappeared down the hall.

The room was bright and formal, smelling of old books and dust and faintly of cigars. Fleur-de-lis wallpaper provided a blue-and-gold backdrop to a massive fireplace mantel with framed photos lined up along its edge: Rittenhour beaming next to his daughter on her wedding day. Four people—Zane guessed it was Rittenhour and his wife and kids when they were young—all decked out in ski gear on a mountain somewhere. A Forbes magazine cover from 2000 on which Rittenhour stood with his arms crossed, looking intense, with the headline "Telecom's Most Powerful Man."

Heavy footsteps marched down the hall.

"Assholes," a voice muttered behind them. Rittenhour appeared in the doorway. He was wearing a black turtleneck sweater and light-wash jeans, what Zane imagined was a tech billionaire uniform since he'd seen it on so many of them in news photos. Rittenhour had added his own twist with black sheepskin slippers lined in puffy black wool, reminding Zane of fuzzy black caterpillars he'd seen at the zoo.

As Rittenhour shut the glass-paneled doors behind him for privacy, a dazzle of lightning strobed in through the windows followed by a boom of thunder. It had a dramatic effect. Rittenhour flicked his cold eyes from Loris to Zane and said, "What do you want to know about Diana Granger?"

"Maybe it's better if we start with what Zane here uncovered," Loris said.

Zane swallowed to try to suppress a growing tickle in his throat. This man made him nervous. "Diana was your research assistant from 1999 until about 2001. She worked closely with you, helping you do research for an autobiography. She vanished from the face of the earth around April 2001, and we can't prove that you continued to keep her on the payroll in some way after that, but there's reason to guess that maybe you did."

"And we've only been working on this for a few days," Loris said. "Just think what else we're going to find if we keep digging."

Zane brought his mobile phone out of his pocket and brought up the digital photo of Dawn to show Rittenhour. "Remember her? This photo was taken a few months before she died. She wasn't Diana Granger then. She was Dawn Renee and her daughter Kayla was twenty-two years old."

The older man didn't even blink those reptilian eyes.

"Who's paying you two? I can only guess who among my many enemies might be interested in trying to embarrass me. But they should know better. I don't embarrass easy. Everyone has some skeletons in the closet from those days. It was a different time. How much are they paying you? What do you want? Twenty thousand dollars? Would that cover it?"

"Come on," Loris said. "There's a million dollars at stake in this case, in Bitcoin anyway. As long as that price holds. And maybe you know where that money came from. The digital currency you sent Dawn, formerly Diana—"

Rittenhour's cursing vocabulary was epic as he unleashed them. His voice must have carried because the woman who answered the door came scurrying down the hall with her mobile phone and peered in at them. Rittenhour waved her away.

"Are you the most incompetent detectives in the world?

You are barely making sense. Are you trying to say there's some tawdry connection between me and Diana and this daughter Kayla? Stupidest thing I've ever heard."

"I don't know about that," Zane said. "I've heard stupider things."

Rittenhour turned his full attention to Zane. "When was the girl born?"

"December 14, 2001."

"Then she was conceived in March 2001, unless the birth was premature or delayed. Was it?"

"Not that we know of," Zane said.

"Get out your notebook and write this down," Rittenhour said.

Loris scoffed at his power play. "Between the two of us, we'll remember whatever it is you're about to say."

"Remember this then. In 1999 I was diagnosed with testicular cancer. We kept it out of the news because I didn't want to spook Wall Street. It was a dicey time in the market. And facing my own mortality was what had me working on that goddamned autobiography. I had cancer treatment that made me infertile starting in mid-1999. My oncologist's name was Gail Dohle, and she works out of Baylor University Medical Center. I'll contact her to let her know you might be calling and to confirm my diagnosis. There's no DNA test needed as far as I'm concerned. And before you can ask, I have an alibi for the night of her murder, and I've communicated that to the police. So, we're done here. Please leave."

He turned and opened the door to the foyer. "Violet!"

The woman came scurrying down the hallway, once again holding her mobile phone at the ready.

"Prepare to dial 911 if these two jackasses don't leave in one minute," he said before marching down the hallway with as much dignity as a man can have in fuzzy black slippers.

Shortly thereafter, Loris pulled into the Waffle House parking lot. It was going to be a long drive home and Loris had said nothing kept her awake quite like Waffle House coffee.

The retro waitress in a wrinkled cotton shirt and bowtie shouted her welcome as Zane and Loris walked into the nearly empty restaurant, and an elderly couple eating in silence checked them out briefly before settling back on their plates. Every Waffle House Zane had seen looked the same: long and narrow like a rail car, split into two halves by a waist-high counter lined with red vinyl stools bolted to the floor. One half of the building was for eating and the other half for the massive grill. Zane slid into one of the booths by the windows. It was warm and smelled like sauteed onions and steak.

The waitress approached, crinkling her eyes at them. "Do you know what you want, or do you need a minute?"

"Coffee," Loris said. "And the T-bone dinner."

Zane grabbed the laminated menu from behind the napkin dispenser and scanned it fast. The menu was sticky under his fingers, undoubtedly with syrup, and this cemented his choice for the restaurant's namesake dish. "I'll have a waffle and two scrambled eggs," he said. "And a Coke."

The waitress left and Zane resisted the urge to check his phone, knowing Loris hated nothing more than people who brought their phones out at the table. It was a weird quirk, considering nearly everyone in the world looked at their phones while waiting for food. But Loris surprised him by placing her phone on the table and opening the voice recorder app.

"Something told me to turn that recorder on before he came in," she said. She hit play and then fast-forward until they heard his voice say once again, "Who's paying you two?"

"Good thing too," Zane said. "Since we weren't about to take notes."

"Not when he orders us to. It was a lousy trip," Loris said.

"I hate guys like that. Entitled, rich. Used to giving orders. Makes me want to do the opposite of whatever they say, even if it's not in my best interests."

"I feel that," Zane said. The waitress delivered the drinks and Zane watched as Loris loaded her coffee up with milk and sugar until it was the color of rusty water.

"I knew a man, a self-made millionaire, who told me money made him feel invincible. Because it solved every problem."

Zane took a swallow of Coke and scowled. "I don't buy it. There's always problems. They're just different ones when you have money."

Loris raised her eyebrows. "I wouldn't know. I've never had that kind of money."

Zane laughed. "Yeah, me neither. I just said that to make me feel better."

When the food was finally in front of them and Zane had chewed and swallowed a quarter of the waffle and two forkfuls of eggs, he told Loris, "I appreciate your showing me the ropes like this. I'm sure it would be easier to work these cases by yourself rather than dragging me along."

"You brought this one in, Zane, so don't sell yourself short. And I'm sorry, but did you just put syrup on your eggs? On purpose?" She made a face.

"Why not? It's a condiment, like ketchup or hot sauce," he said. "Anyway, tell me what you thought of him. I'm curious if my observations stack up with yours."

They went through the encounter almost word for word, pausing only to take a few more bites of their meals. By the time they got to Rittenhour's threat to call 911, Zane's plate was empty and all that was left of Loris's steak and hashbrowns was the T-bone and a smear of ketchup. Loris had finished two cups of coffee as well.

Zane swallowed the last bite of waffle. "He's probably not

Kayla's father. Since he offered us the doctor's name to check it. Unless he's paid off the doctor because rich people have the money to do things like that."

"Something about the way he said it makes me think it's true, but we'll still have to check it out. And I suppose there's a chance he could have had his sperm frozen before that happened and then had her impregnated through IVF. I mean, the technology is there but it doesn't seem likely."

"Right. If he had gone to all that trouble to get her pregnant, wouldn't he have done everything he could to stay in the child's life?"

"Unless something bad happened between them. We certainly need to check out what that doctor has to say."

"I feel like I should have uncovered that cancer diagnosis in my searches. We might have had a better sense of what we were walking into if I had," Zane said.

"Don't beat yourself up about it. We learned something during that visit that Rittenhour didn't want us to learn."

"What was that?"

"That he was ready for us. He confirmed he knew that date of birth."

"How did he do that? I'm not following."

"The way he was ready with those dates and his doctor's information. He had arranged that story in his head before we came. He'd probably been thinking about it since we first saw him in Tulsa."

"Uh-huh." Zane tipped his glass to his mouth to crunch on a piece of ice. "Thanks for the encouragement. Do we tell Kayla about Rittenhour's reaction?"

"Not yet." Loris glanced at the old-fashioned watch on her wrist. "We've got to get on the road if we want to make it home before two in the morning."

"What do you think Rittenhour's relationship to Dawn was if he wasn't her lover? Is he the one behind the Bitcoin?"

"God only knows. There could be a thousand reasons why Dawn didn't want to talk to him in that restaurant. And we have no idea if that cryptocurrency is related to her death or just another weird mystery. But it was interesting, wasn't it, how prepared he was to talk about how he wasn't Kayla's father?"

"His son," Zane said. "What if his son is Kayla's father and Rittenhour is the grandfather?"

"Maybe. I can't shake the feeling that this Rittenhour is in the middle of it all: the murder and the money. So tomorrow you've got two things to run down. The doctor, which you can do on the phone since Rittenhour is paving the way there, and the son. We need to research him a bit more, so we know how to approach."

"Three things. We need to find out more about Tyler Swinton too. Figure out how he's related to all this and why he's decided to connect with Kayla the way he did."

"Definitely. The big hurdle is that we don't know when she changed from Diana Granger to Dawn Renee. Maybe your internet friend will remember something else about Diana's relationship with the son, Curtis. Right now, she's the only person we have who knew Diana back then, except for the Rittenhours and maybe Swinton."

The drive back was spent talking through what to do next. All they had was three names, a photograph, two workplaces, a chance encounter at a restaurant, and a random person on the Internet who knew Diana way back when. They didn't even know if during those long-ago months, Dawn/Diana had lived among seven hundred thousand people in Fort Worth, or in the greater Dallas area with another three million people—or even in Arlington. They had the names of only four people who had known her back then for sure: the Rittenhours, father and son and maybe the daughter, and Derrick from WorthComm. The daughter was a bit of a stretch, but Derrick had said she had met Diana at the Rittenhour mansion so maybe the daughter had some information. They put her on the list but not a top priority. Derrick had said she told Zane all she knew about Diana but something new might occur to her, so it was worth a recheck. It wasn't a promising start. Zane updated Kayla Renee, who agreed that they could post some ads on Twitter and Facebook.

Tuesday morning, he did that, working on the wording with Loris:

$2,000 reward for any verifiable information regarding the whereabouts and movements of Diana Granger aka Dawn Renee between June 1999 and June 2001.

Zane attached the photo to the posts and boosted both to people in the states of Texas and Oklahoma, but not without an argument from Loris about the wisdom of advertising it to anyone in the United States. Zane's objection was that casting such a wide net would flood them with responses from opportunists grabbing at the money and he would have to follow some of them up even though most would be dead ends, and of those, a fair amount would develop into pests. Zane won.

It was five o'clock when Zane sat across from Derrick at No Place again. She looked like she'd gotten a head start on the drinking today; her whole face was relaxed, her mouth ready to smile and her toes tapping to the Deep Purple song "Smoke on the Water" banging out its three-chord progression through the speakers. Must be nice to relax with a beer after a hard day of trolling WorthComm online.

She blinked at Zane and said she hoped this wouldn't take too long. "I'll be blunt. I've had a long day and I want to chill out. I assume this is about Rittenhour."

Zane nodded. "Yes and no. With Sherwood, we hit a dead end. He's got an alibi for the night of her death that the police say is solid. And it looks like he's not the father of Dawn Renee's daughter."

"What?" Derrick's mouth stayed open. "You know for sure?"

"Yeah. I won't go into it for confidentiality reasons, but we're pretty sure he's not the one."

"His cancer diagnosis, right? He had testicular cancer sometime in the early 2000s," Derrick said. "Didn't I tell you that?"

Zane shook his head. "No, but I didn't ask you about anything like that either. Didn't occur to me. I wish I had. Rittenhour said he was diagnosed in 1999. That was why he was working on the autobiography. He thought it would be his legacy project. We're going to check on the diagnosis, but it looks like he physically could not be the father. Unless you know he might be lying."

"What was the date of birth again?"

"December 4, 2001."

"It tracks. The rumors were he got that diagnosis sometime in early 1999, with treatment following. He hid it because the stock price was on a phenomenal run, I'm guessing. He didn't want to spook the market. I can ask my friends on the Worth-Comm subreddit what they know about it if you want."

"Not necessary. But you told me when we met last that you had once thought it possible that something was developing between Diana and Curtis, Rittenhour's son. He was thirty-eight years old then and I'm guessing he was working at Worth-Comm. So perhaps Rittenhour was supporting Dawn Renee not because she was the mother of his child. Perhaps she was the mother of his grandchild. What do you think?"

"Did I say that?" She frowned and took a long swig of beer.

Zane nodded.

"I must have been spitballing."

"You seemed pretty sure."

"Look, I was happy to provide information, especially publicly available information, that reflected poorly on old Rittenhour. He's a dog. He deserves what he gets. God knows he has made enough trouble for me but I'm not going to get into that with you. Still, I'm not going to volunteer information to get Curtis in trouble, even if I had any. I have a high regard for Curtis. I'd even call him a friend in a way. But I will tell you this—because anybody would tell you this. For the past decade or so, Curtis Rittenhour and his mad dog of a father haven't been on speaking terms. My opinion of Sherwood Rittenhour is mild compared to his. Of course, with him it's more personal, father and son. Runs deep. If Sherwood was trying to help Diana or even talk to her, it wasn't on account of his son, if you ask me."

She drained her beer and signaled the bartender for another. "I'm done talking about Curtis," she said. "But if you need more information about Sherwood, I'd be happy to help. Frankly, I would like to see him hurt. I know it's an awful thing to say. But I'm not the only one. Maybe that money came from him for blackmail? Did Diana know something that would hurt him? If so, I hope you uncover it. In fact... if you need money to finance that—"

"We have a client. We're not looking for another one," Zane said. The idea of using his investigative skills to root out information just to wreak revenge on someone turned his stomach. He had frittered away enough time. He thanked her for meeting with him and left the bar.

He called Loris from the car. "I call that navigating a maze with no cheese," he said before he filled her in on the conversation. "Complete time waste. Maybe Curtis is Kayla's father.

And old Sherwood might be interested in knowing his grand-daughter."

"Yup, maybe so," Loris said. "I'll stick with running down the mysterious Tyler Swinton and you take on Curtis. He was older than Diana, right? Was he married?"

"I'll start digging when I get back in the office," Zane said.

Chapter 15
Zane

The trouble with putting out requests for information on social media was weeding out the garbage. Some were just trolls, spewing anger into the world one tweet and direct message at a time. Saying the kinds of things to people they'd never dare to say face-to-face, but they felt empowered to do so from behind their keyboard or their phone. Some were so screwed-up Zane only kept them because he had been trained to retain everything related to a job until it was finished. One was from a weirdo who said Diana Granger was an alien from planet Memax, and though Zane had never ruled out life on other planets, he thought it more likely she was from Arlington.

One message got his attention quickly that Wednesday morning. It was an email reply from Curtis Rittenhour. Zane had found his email online and written:

Dear Mr. Rittenhour:

On behalf of a client, I need information regarding the activities and associates of Diana Granger during the years 1999 to

2001 when she was working for your father. I have been told you may be able to help with some information.

Zane had given his email address and cell phone number and Curtis Rittenhour had replied.

All it said was:

I haven't heard that name in years. I doubt I can be of any help to you but if you can give me a call later today around four p.m.

Zane wrote back that he got the message and that time worked and he appreciated the reply.

He drove home for lunch at eleven-thirty. He was feeling restless and worried about the state of his relationship with Tiffany. Her hurt feelings over him taking the case with Kayla without telling her had diminished but not evaporated entirely. She was just a little bit distant last night and this morning. He loved Tiffany and he'd told her so again and again. He wanted her to be sure of his love. But if he were honest with himself, he needed some reassurance too. She had been a bit preoccupied with the store since deciding to buy it, constantly worrying about money and trying different marketing techniques on social media to drive more sales. But he didn't want to discourage her from that work by complaining how neglected he felt. He just hoped she would realize that she needed to find a healthier work/life balance without him having to ask her.

He heard laughter from inside the home and opened the door to survey the scene. Verda, Emmaline, and some guy sat at the dining table laughing over bowls of chili and slices of ham. Emmaline bounced up when she saw him and pointed to the guy, who was coincidentally named Guy. He looked like the kind of jerk who live-streamed his ice cream orders at Braum's and was mean to the counter staff.

Zane caught Verda's eye and saw that she was sitting bolt upright—not as relaxed or jovial as her laugh would indicate.

Guy rose from the table and crossed the living room to shake Zane's hand. "I've heard so much about you," he said. "A detective, huh?"

Zane nodded.

Guy smiled, revealing plenty of evidence of the chili he had just eaten in his crooked teeth. His breath smelled corrosive and overheated. At first glance, Zane had thought he was in his early twenties, but he quickly revised that upward by ten years. He wore a Megadeath T-shirt underneath a black-and-gold plaid flannel shirt and jeans that pooled around his feet like elephant legs. His brown curls were gelled and stiff as an insect caught in amber. Emmaline hugged Verda and said something about having to get moving.

"Don't leave on my account," Zane said.

"We've stayed too long," Emmaline said. "We just dropped by, and your grandma tempted us with chili." They stood making brief small talk for a moment, but Zane couldn't help wondering what had transpired with Verda before he arrived. Verda liked everybody but her stiffness and over-the-top politeness made it clear that something was off with Guy.

When they finally left, Verda cleared their plates from the table and filled a fresh bowl with chili for Zane. She set the bowl on the table and then sat across from him, folding her hands in front of her. She definitely had something to say.

"So, Emmaline has a new friend," Zane said.

"He's slicker than greased owl poop. Where did she find this one? I met him once before at the mailbox and I didn't like him then either. Lettie met him too and had the same impression. Emmaline must be losing her mind to be bringing him around here."

"Where did he come from?"

"He's renting a room from Mrs. Ahern. Emmaline must be slower than molasses on a cold day to not see through this clown. There's something off with his eyes. A coldness deep down. He tries to cover it up. What do you think he wants with her?"

"Probably what most people want with her. She's beautiful, she's funny and smart. She can be kind sometimes too," Zane said.

"Oh, don't tell me you're still carrying a torch for her too," Verda said.

"No, no, not me. I'm over that."

"I just don't see what she wants with him," Verda said.

"Everyone gets lonely," Zane said. "Maybe he has some good qualities that you didn't see."

"I didn't get to be sixty-three years old without knowing a thing or two about people. He's up to no good. I'm going to call Mrs. Ahern. What's the matter with her, renting to a man like that?"

Times were tough and people at the Majestic always needed money, so Zane didn't give too much thought to why Mrs. Ahern rented a room to Emmaline's new love interest. It didn't matter. As he walked to his car to head back to the office, he thought he could hear the muffled sounds of Guy's voice from the Perrymans' driveway, rising and falling, complaining about something. He couldn't make out the words, but the tone was clear... testy and impatient.

Maybe Emmaline would come to share Verda and Lettie's opinion that Guy was not as nice as he pretended to be. Or maybe not. People make fools of themselves all the time in the name of love or lust. And he didn't need to be in the full-time business of rescuing Emmaline from every bad choice. He was tired of it, and it would only make Tiffany more jealous. He didn't need anything else coming between them. He drove back to the office with a full belly. His call to Tiffany rang ten times before slipping to voicemail. Her voice came on with a teasing greeting: "I don't listen to voicemail but leave one if you want." The joke seemed harsh in light of the tension between them. He hung up at the beep without saying a word.

Back at the office, Zane spent most of the next three hours finding out a few things about Curtis Rittenhour. He had married a woman named Alexis Belleville in June 1989 and divorced her in 1995. He waited until 2015 to get remarried, this time to a man named George Playford and this second time seemed to take. No record of divorce. Curtis became a vice president of Prosperity Financial Bank in 2012. He graduated from Baylor University in 1985 and he had been on a fundraising committee for the Baylor alumni association in 2004. If he had children, Zane couldn't find any evidence of them online but sometimes that was the case. Some people loved to post photos of their kids meeting every childhood milestone on social media, others kept it pretty quiet. Curtis Rittenhour and his husband kept silent on social media unless they were using aliases he hadn't uncovered yet.

Zane figured he'd learn more by talking to Curtis and laying eyes on him, and he was right. He logged onto the Microsoft Teams meeting link that Curtis's secretary had sent over and studied the man's face on the computer screen as Zane thanked him for taking the time and reintroduced himself. He had a hard time keeping the man focused even during this short opening exchange. There was no resemblance to his father at all, especially around the eyes. Where Sherwood Rittenhour's eyes had been flinty and reptilian, Curtis's were as soft and brown and good-natured as a puppy dogs. Although he seemed to look straight into the camera, Zane had the feeling Curtis was seeing something else, maybe a beach he wanted to be on or a fancy meal he wanted to eat. Zane tried to keep an open mind. However, first impressions were powerful, and this man certainly gave off the impression of a dreamer first, vice president second. It was impossible to gauge his height or build on the video screen. If Zane had to guess from the video screen, the man was broad-shouldered and average sized. He sat in one of those webbed black office armchairs in a white button-up shirt and no tie.

"A private investigator, huh? That's an interesting job. Snooping around in people's lives."

Zane frowned. Curtis was trying to throw him off balance. This wasn't a good start to the conversation.

"I'd describe it differently. People come to us for information and answers to tough questions. I'd say we help people."

"Depends on the perspective, I suppose. Some people want information, others don't want to give it. Secrets are what drives this world, don't you think? Even in this age of information and transparency, secrets are necessary."

Zane didn't want to fall into a philosophical argument with this guy. "Truth usually comes out anyway. Sometimes we just make it happen faster," he said.

Curtis nodded. "Have you ever seen that movie, *Secrets and Lies* from 1996? There's a great line from it. Something like: 'Secrets and lies! We're all in pain! Why can't we share our pain?' Well, the reason for the secrets and the pain in that movie is resentments. Long-standing, harsh resentments resulting from years and years of actions and inactions and small slights. And that, Mr. Private Investigator, is what happened between me and my father too. God knows I've tried to get along with him. I bring it up because I know what you want. Derrick has told me about Diana Granger's murder and your questions about me. And I'd be happy to discuss my father with you more, but your email asked about Diana Granger so I'd like to tidy that up for you."

"I'm listening," Zane said.

"You thought my father may have killed Diana Granger or

fathered a child with her and now you've learned those are less likely than a unicorn joining this call. So now you've decided that I'm either a killer or Diana's lover or both."

"I wouldn't say we've decided. I'd say we are inquiring."

Curtis waved his hand on the screen as though brushing away a fly. "The year 2001 was during the time I was trying to produce a film called *Reconciliation.* That's when I met George. It wasn't that long ago but it still seems like the stone ages in some ways. I kept him a secret for years. But he changed my life."

"I saw you're married now."

"As soon as that Supreme Court ruling made same-sex marriage in Texas possible, we jumped at the chance. My father has never forgiven me. But you don't care about that. What you want to know is where was I on the date of Diana Granger's death. I was in Fort Worth, at a fundraiser until midnight. Dozens of people can attest to it. And next, you want to know if I fathered a child with Diana Granger in 2001, correct? The answer is no. I knew her as my father's research assistant, nothing more."

"You get that I'd be a fool to just take you at your word for that," Zane said.

"I understand. That's why I'd be happy to take a DNA test to prove it. More than happy to. You just point me to a lab here in Fort Worth and I'll get it done. But you said you wanted information about Diana. Ask me anything else about her, but I doubt if I know anything that will help. According to Derrick, she changed her name to Dawn Renee, gave birth to a daughter who is twenty-two years old now, and fled Fort Worth."

"Just about."

"I can see why you'd think there was a WorthComm connection. Just because of the timing. Then I need to rethink a thing or two about dear old dad. This is surprising to me. My father is very big on meeting his responsibilities, but the thing is, only he decides what those responsibilities are. And let me tell you, he moves that goal post all the time. Derrick said that it seemed like blackmail to her, but I can't imagine that mean old buzzard submitting to blackmail. There's some cryptocurrency involved somehow?"

Loris strode into the room just then and flung her bag on her desk.

"Bitcoin, on a hard wallet, and worth about a million dollars," Zane said. He grabbed a slip of paper and wrote Curtis Rittenhour's name on it, holding it up for Loris to see, just out of camera range.

Curtis laughed. "That's ridiculous to think my father would be involved in that. Dad thinks cryptocurrency is the biggest Ponzi scheme yet. You've got to be joking. And did Diana, or I guess Dawn as she was calling herself, say where the money came from?"

Zane shook his head.

Loris leaned against her desk, chin down and eyes wide open as she stared at some distant point on the industrial carpet. Zane knew she was listening intently but resisting the urge to jump into the conversation. It would only confuse things with Curtis to bring a second person in at this point.

"Ridiculous. Unbelievable. When was the crypto bought? That should be easy to find out. And who knows? The way things are going it might be worthless again soon." Curtis ran his fingers through his hair and leaned into the camera. "I don't do anything at the bank, you know. Dad installed a bank president and told him to keep me out of any important decisions once I married George. But I've stayed on to spite my father and he won't fire me because he's stubborn as hell. He wants Prosperity Bank to stay in the family, and I don't know, maybe he's waiting around for me to be done with my 'gay phase,' as he calls it. But I've had some good ideas and he knows it so that's another reason. I saw the Internet of things—you know, refrigerators and cars and baby monitors with sensors and software—coming long before he did and told him that WorthComm should get involved in mobile broadband uses. I'm a big picture guy and I've got to tell you I've never wanted to see the big picture more than I do right now. What was my father up to?"

Zane was losing patience and maybe Loris was too, since she puffed up her checks like a chipmunk and blew out a long breath. He could already see the steps ahead: they'd get the DNA test, but he had a feeling they already knew the answer. This guy was an exasperating blowhard, but Zane didn't think he was lying. And checking alibis was something the Tulsa police was better suited for.

He got off the call as fast as he could. When a Microsoft Teams window popped up with a survey question about how the call quality was, he pounded the thumbs-down symbol more times than necessary. He knew the software was just asking about the connection, but he wanted to have some place to spend his frustration.

"Don't punish the keyboard," Loris said.

Zane filled her in on the tiny bit of information he'd gotten from Curtis before she walked in. He threw his hands up in a gesture of giving up. "I don't know what to do next. Tell me you found something interesting about Tyler Swinton."

"Kind of a lot of nothing," she said. "I did figure out his Tulsa connection though, that might explain why he was up here hanging out at the Boot Barn."

"He comes up here for the medical marijuana," Zane said.

Loris laughed. "Close. His wife's parents live here. And they are investors in his new company. According to the corporate filings, they own half the shares."

"All right, so he has a legitimate reason to be here and maybe meeting Kayla at the Boot Barn was just a fluke."

"He does have a reputation for chasing younger women though. There's a sexual harassment lawsuit that was filed against him at his previous start-up. Kind of the same set-up: met a young woman at a coffee shop, hired her as a social media coordinator, then got a little *hands-on*, if you know what I mean. I talked to her today. She settled out of court and wouldn't discuss the details too much, but I got enough."

"Either way, it's good that Kayla is staying at your uncle's. Just until things settle down. It's like we're inching forward."

"Sometimes we just need to wait. Either for the next idea or for something to happen," Loris said.

"Patience is not my virtue," Zane said.

Chapter 16
Zane

The following Monday, Loris and Zane sat in the office stumped for words. They still were at an impasse, but they were further down the road, albeit a different road than they thought.

First, to answer the question of Sherwood Rittenhour's fertility Zane had to install some fancy telemedicine software on his computer to talk remotely to Gail Dohle, M.D. of the Baylor University Medical Center, a frustrating process that took the better part of an hour because of the computer's limited memory and Zane's limited tech skills. Why did everything these days involve setting up a password and clicking dozens of preferences? All these website prompts about accepting cookies made him hungry.

When he finally connected with the oncologist, his computer screen showed him a grey-haired woman with shaggy black eyebrows and a tired wide mouth, sitting at a desk in an office. He could hear the soft click click of keyboard typing and waited a few minutes before she was done and gave him her attention.

"Are you Zane Clearwater?"

"Yes."

"Since this information is confidential, I just want to make sure. Do you have a driver's license or something you could show me?"

Zane fished his wallet out of his pocket and held the laminated license up to the camera. Dr. Dohle leaned in for a look and then nodded.

"We squeezed you in because Mr. Rittenhour said it was urgent. He asked me to confirm his statement to you that he is infertile and has been for more than twenty years. I confirm it. That is true."

"If you don't mind, we want it airtight. You know it for a fact?"

"I wouldn't say such a thing if I didn't know it. Multiple examinations and analyses, over time, for years."

"Around March 2001, then. He was infertile then?"

"Yes. Most assuredly so. Mr. Rittenhour didn't tell me what this was about. If this is a paternity suit, it's ridiculous. I'd be glad to testify." Her cell phone trilled, and she glanced down. "I've got to take this."

Zane thanked her again and hung up the call. So much for Sherwood Rittenhour as the father. He called Baylor University Medical Center and confirmed Dr. Dohle's credentials then double-checked the photo of her with a screenshot he took from their call and it all matched. That really did finish off old Sherwood as Daddy dearest, at least until they got a hold of the DNA testing for Curtis Rittenhour and Kayla Renee.

The DNA lab's conclusion said this: "The alleged father cannot be excluded as the biological father of the tested child. Based on the analysis of the STR loci listed above, the probability of paternity is 99.7869913%. However, a mutation was found, and this does not exclude close relatives such as a brother, uncle, or a father. This is as compared to an untested, unrelated, random individual of the Caucasian population."

It was the first real break they'd had in the case, and it gave Zane a tingle at the bottom of his spine. By God, they had proof. Actual proof that these two slippery Rittenhour men were related to Kayla. But to be conclusive, the DNA lab wanted to do more tests—of Diana/Dawn, of Sherwood, of Sherwood's other offspring, Caroline. The police still had custody of Dawn's body so they might be interested in the testing, but Sherwood and his daughter seemed like a long shot unless the police compelled them to do so. So, Zane called Old Spice.

The detective was at his office and would see Zane. Loris was on the phone trying to convince an insurance adjuster that someone was probably faking their claim when Zane took off for downtown Tulsa.

The Tulsa Police Detective Division where Detective Angus Pastor worked was a vast dark space filled with desks about ten feet apart. Empty chairs rested against desk fronts covered in paperwork and clutter. The place had the feel of an airport, a place where people gathered temporarily and hoped not to stay too long. Zane knew for a fact that most of the action happened outside these walls in interrogation rooms hidden from view or on the streets and in homes and restaurants and offices. The tang of sweat, adrenaline, and metal permeated the air.

A black vape stick sat on the corner of his desk next to a framed photo of his granddaughter. Zane knew the police detective had given up the Marlboro Reds to appease his kids, but he wasn't sure that vaping was all that healthy either. He sat on the wooden chair at the end of the desk while Old Spice finished talking on the phone. When he hung up and settled back in his chair, Zane said, "I've got news that might help in that murder we were talking about."

Old Spice hammed it up. He probed, "Which murder is that? I'm up to my ears."

"A woman named Dawn Renee was poisoned in her home and—"

"Oh yes, that one. So, you want some more information from me, I'm guessing."

Zane nodded. "And you think we may have some information you want, which is why you agreed to see me, right? I'll cut to the chase. Dawn Renee used to be known as Diana Granger from Arlington, Texas, where she worked closely with Sherwood Rittenhour, the CEO of the third largest telecom company in the world and one of the richest men if you believe those online lists. She was friendly with his son, Curtis. But right around the time Kayla was getting ready to be born, Diana changed her name and moved to Tulsa."

Old Spice rocked forward in the chair and placed his elbows on the desk. His hands propped up his chin and covered his mouth, so Zane couldn't see if he was smiling or not, but his eyes glinted with surprise and interest.

"And about a month ago, Dawn practically fled a restaurant in Fort Worth because Sherwood Rittenhour came up to talk to her. He says he's got an alibi for the night of the murder. Not to say he couldn't have hired someone. He has the resources. He thinks we're blackmailers trying to say that Kayla is his daughter. His son Curtis probably does too. But Curtis is the one who agreed to a DNA test and the results seem to match the Rittenhour family tree without pointing to exactly who. Sherwood had testicular cancer in the late 1990s and his doctor says it can't be him."

"Interesting. So, Kayla's part of the Rittenhour tree? And

you want us to run some DNA tests on her mother to find out more?"

Zane tried to contain his excitement. "That's what we're thinking."

Old Spice scratched some words down in the notebook on his desk. "Yeah, it makes sense. I'll look into the Rittenhours a bit more. And I'll let them know they have you to thank."

"They know that already, I'm sure. Sherwood Rittenhour is no fan of ours, but you probably guessed that anyway. Anything on Tyler Swinton?"

"He's being a bit elusive. I've asked someone on the Fort Worth police to go to his office and ask a few questions."

"Like where he was the night of Dawn's murder?"

Old Spice waved him away and didn't even bother to answer the question.

Loris and Zane headed over to Pickert Real Estate to take another shot at Pickert. The real estate developer's first remark when they entered the office was that Zane and Loris had the kind of tenacity he liked to see on a job. He said he was always looking for hard-working talent and asked if they considered working in real estate development. Zane had to smile when he saw Loris rub her lips with a knuckle to keep from responding negatively about how she only worked for herself. Pickert was helpful to them in this case, and they didn't want to offend him.

"Real estate is mainly problem-solving and leverage," Pickert said. "Ferreting out facts and knowing how to use them."

"Not right now," Loris said. "We're fully booked with clients, including working for Kayla Renee. And on behalf of her, thank you for seeing us again. I know you don't think you have any more information for us that can help, but you'd be surprised how often we find that people have knowledge of facts without being aware of their significance. I once questioned a man for five hours on little details and finally got a fact that solved a crime."

"I don't have five hours," Pickert said. "I can give you thirty minutes. And speaking of facts, you knew something I didn't, judging from those Facebook ads everyone's been seeing. Dawn Renee was an alias. What was her name again? Denise Strongman?"

"Diana Granger," Zane said, shifting position in the plush leather chair to avoid the afternoon sun shining through the windows and into his eyes.

"I thought Renee was her married name all this time. I never asked though. But why would she change her first name?"

"We have to keep some information confidential, Mr. Pickert," Loris said. Her tone was clipped. She hated when interviewees tried to turn the tables.

"But you're stuck, right? That's why you're back talking to me."

"Correct," Loris said.

"It seems like the police are looking into this adequately. Are you just wasting Kayla's money? I feel like I should look out for her interests out of respect for her mother," Pickert said. It sounded like a lie to Zane. He was just trying to bully Loris. Good luck with that.

"Kayla is glad to have us doing what we're doing. We just wanted to check back in with you and ask a few questions. Who was Dawn close to at the company?"

Pickert raised his hand into a stop sign gesture aimed at Loris. "That's absurd. I don't think anyone who works here was involved in her murder. Nobody had anything beyond professional relationships with her. Nobody. Not even me. We had some meals together sometimes, but it was always about business. She was immensely private almost to the point of rudeness. I can give you names of her co-workers, the ones she worked with every day, but it's a dead end. The police have already interviewed everyone."

"We get that. We'll take the names, and we understand that this kind of inquiry often leads nowhere. It's part of the job. Let's try another avenue. When and where did you see Dawn for the last time?"

"That day she died, around noon at the office. Like I said before, I was getting ready to travel with the family to Branson for a long weekend."

Loris wrote in her notebook, letting the pause build for a few moments. Zane decided to jump in with a question of his own. "Did she say anything about her plans for that evening?"

Pickert turned to Zane, his jawline hard and his tone sharp. "Yes. She was going to upgrade some servers or something, do it at night when no one was there."

Zane leaned forward, maintaining strong eye contact. He wasn't going to be intimidated. He had a job to do. "Did everyone know she was going to work late?"

"I don't know what they knew but they probably guessed it. It wasn't uncommon for her to work late. I think folks would have been surprised if she *didn't* work late. She liked working in the quiet off-hours. She said it relaxed her though I never thought of her as relaxed."

Loris changed tactics and Zane was enjoying how well they were working together. The flow was there. "Let's go back earlier that day. Did you spend time with her in the morning?"

Pickert leaned back in his chair, eyes on the ceiling as though trying to remember. "Not much. Someone had brought in donuts and bagels and that kind of thing, and everyone gathered for a little bit in the break room. She didn't stay long because someone came by to see her."

"Who came?"

"A woman from one of the software vendors, I think. Just routine. Something to do with the upgrades planned later that night. I never paid much attention to the computer nerd chatter. Later, I stopped by to see if she could help me with a phone operating system upgrade. The phone kept saying I was out of storage or something and I counted on her to fix it. I know that probably my kids or anyone in this office could help me with something so basic, but she was always happy to do it for me. She didn't talk down to me or laugh at me for not understanding the technology. She was remarkable that way. Over the years she got a few offers to join other firms, other more technological firms too, but she turned them all down."

"Why was that, do you think?"

"I don't really know but I was grateful. I surmised that she liked the complete freedom she had working for me."

"Except when you sent her to Fort Worth," Zane said.

"Yes, except then."

Loris glanced at Zane and then back at Pickert. "What if I asked you to tell me everything she said to you that morning? Could you do it?"

Pickert smiled as though Loris had made a lame joke. "No, not at all. Anyway, it was just the usual stuff. I don't remember any hint of what was going to happen to her that night."

Pickert slid open a desk drawer. Zane thought he was going to pull out his phone and start texting or something, but instead, the older man brought out a flask and took a long hit. Zane could smell the antiseptic zest of hard liquor from across the desk, an alcoholic's sixth sense. He offered the flask to Loris and Zane, but they waved him off.

"Suit yourself. I thought it might grease up the memory

some," Pickert said. And it did grease up his memory as well as his willingness to spend more time with them. Thirty minutes ticked by into an hour, then an hour and a half. Pickert took them through the day's work events, using a print-out of his calendar as a guide, then the day before, and then it hit.

Pickert was going through the Wednesday routine and telling them how he and Dawn had been on their way out to have lunch with somebody when the receptionist stopped them and told Dawn that some man had been there trying to reach her and he had had to threaten to call the police if he didn't leave. The receptionist had said he thought the man might be waiting for them in the parking lot. Dawn had thanked him, and they left through the back door and got into Pickert's car. Loris asked what the man's name was, but Pickert knew nothing about him. He had figured he was an over-zealous salesperson because there were a lot of those and didn't give it another thought.

Zane almost didn't make the connection. His mind was in slow-motion mode because the trivialities of daily life at Pickert Real Estate were hardly scintillating, but the hunch came to him and he couldn't wait to test out the idea. He sat up straighter and must have looked more alert and awake.

"Did you see the man?" he asked Pickert. At this point, Pickert's flask must have been half empty and he shook his head slowly. Loris noticed Zane's energy shift, looked at her watch, and said maybe it was time to wrap things up for now.

"Can we chat with the receptionist?" Zane asked.

Pickert nodded and walked them to the front desk where a man in his twenties with a mouthful of bright white teeth and curly brown hair sat talking on a headset. They stood patiently while he finished giving directions to someone.

"This is Eric," Pickert said, ending the name in a slurry cough.

If it was unusual that Pickert was fried in the middle of the day, Eric didn't let on. He simply looked up at the threesome with a wide smile and asked how he could help.

Zane searched in his phone's web browser for Tyler Swinton, finding his photo easily on the Valor Medicine for Men webpage. He zoomed in on his face and showed Eric his phone. "Have you ever seen this man before?"

"Yes. That's the man who had been trying to see Dawn. The one who got so angry," Eric said. "He had said his name was Phil Mickelson."

Pickert laughed out loud. "The professional golfer? Let me see that picture."

"I've never heard of Phil Mickelson before," Eric said. "I thought that was his name."

"That's not Phil Mickelson," Pickert said, handing the phone back to Zane.

"His name is Tyler Swinton," Zane said.

"Yeah, I saw that in his bio there," Pickert said.

"Did you tell the police about him?" Zane asked.

"Of course," Eric said. "But I told them his name was Phil Mickelson. I'm not sure the person who interviewed me knew who that was either. I mean, the only golfer I know is Tiger Woods."

"Is Martina Decomo here?" Zane's hunches were working on overtime now. He felt so much energy it was as if he'd put his finger in an electrical socket.

Eric punched some buttons on the desk phone in front of him. "Martina, can you come up to the front desk? Mr. Pickert and the detectives are asking for you," he said, a pleasant smile in his voice. Zane wondered if his own voice always sounded like it had a scowl in it. He hated talking on the phone. Texting was so much easier.

Pickert collapsed into one of the upholstered chairs in the

entrance foyer and picked up a copy of *Architectural Digest* magazine from the nearby table. "Do we actually subscribe to this?" he asked Eric.

Eric shrugged. "It comes every month, so I guess so."

The click-clack of heels on tile announced Martina's arrival. She sparkled as she stepped into the sunlit foyer, her metallic-threaded red knit dress and matching blazer gleaming like a thousand stars. She held out a hand with long, pointy nails to Zane and Loris. "Good to see you both again," she said. "What's up?"

Zane held the phone up again. "Have you seen this man before?"

"That's the other man from the steakhouse," Martina said.

Chapter 17
Lettie

Angel was frenetically happy after the latest meeting with Atomic Games. Even though he had been working with them two-and-a-half months, he viewed all the hours of live streaming, the earning of sponsorships, and the brainstorming sessions about content creation and video game marketing as prelude to bigger and better things on an endless staircase upwards. After hundreds of hours of nonstop shilling for Atomic Video Games and the pressure of a baby who went through thirty dollars of diapers a day, he was ready to start his life as an influencer with a capital "I" and get the money he thought came with that. He was completely focused on this next chapter and the riches he saw almost within his grasp.

Lettie wasn't so sure. She sat on the bed, looking beyond Milly's crib and out the window, watching smoke wafting up toward the sun from someone's barbecue.

Dreams were good, Lettie had told him over and over. Dreams and goals gave them something to look toward. But the way Angel was completely consumed by this path was unsettling. It was like he had tunnel vision and this path was the only way forward. All around them was evidence that hoping for the one good thing that would change everything was nonsense. Mrs. Ahern and her weekly scratcher tickets, Emmaline hoping for her big break, Verda and her thrift store scrounging, sure each day would be the day she'd uncover treasure. Dreams were good but no substitute for understanding reality. And Lettie was nothing if not logical. So many of life's outcomes were outside your control. But Angel wanted nothing more than he wanted to move into this house in Oklahoma City for two months and make content for Atomic Games full-time. He seemed incapable of grasping why Lettie did not see the attraction and he was trying everything to change her mind in the last forty-eight hours before Wednesday's deadline. He paced back and forth in the room like an excited child.

"You've never been there, honey. Coming to visit me will be like a vacation! And the documentary filming only lasts two months. That's nothing. It will be over before you know it."

"But I can't stay at the house with you, and neither can Milly. What would we do? Have Verda or Zane get us a hotel room or something? Anyway, how are we going to afford that? And she's changing so much every day. You're going to miss things. You won't even know what you'll miss."

"Two months, that's it, Lettie. It will go fast."

"Don't you see how it's going to be more than that? It's a test. They're testing you out. And you're going to do well. You're going to amaze them. Then it will be another two months and another and another."

Angel smiled. "Why is that a bad thing? You should want that for me. For us. Everything I'm doing is for us."

"You forget that I've seen you during the full-time streaming days. I've seen how consuming it is. How tired you get. Meanwhile, I'll be taking care of Milly by myself because you'll want me to move to Oklahoma City and away from my grandma and brother. What is there for me in Oklahoma City besides online school and childcare? You need to find an opportunity here in Tulsa so we can be supported by family and friends. The network we've built. It takes a village to raise a child."

"There are good people in Oklahoma City just like there are in Tulsa. Picture this—I'm a success and I get a year or two-year contract. We buy a house! Can you imagine—a house of our own. With granite countertops and a gaming room and a big king-sized bed. Milly has her own room and there's enough space for Verda and Zane and Tiffany to come and visit anytime they want."

"How do two sixteen-year-olds buy a house?"

"Let me finish. We get married at one of those big old-fashioned churches with a white steeple—"

Lettie could feel her heat gauge rising into the red zone and she interrupted again. "Picture this. You decline this opportunity and guess what—Atomic Video Games keeps you on contract and you get to work from Tulsa. It turns out the Oklahoma City thing didn't matter. I love you, Angel, and I will make compromises for you, but you can't act like this doesn't impact me. There will be other opportunities."

"Atomic Games is looking for my answer by Wednesday. You know that."

He wasn't even hearing her anymore. She didn't know what else to say so she decided to be as direct as she could.

"You can tell them right now that you decline." Lettie glanced at Milly in her crib, miraculously staying asleep through her parents' argument, grabbed her keys from the dresser, and told Angel she was going out for some fresh air. Outside, she put her hands over her face and started to cry. She was exhausted and nothing was easy. Nothing. So, she put one foot in front of the other and started walking toward the Majestic's mailroom.

She turned the corner and saw Emmaline coming toward her with Guy Callahan. They were walking hip to hip, arms entwined. He was a good foot taller than her and nearly double her size in width. Emmaline looked flushed with happiness, that special glow people get when they're falling in love. Not the vibe Lettie was looking for at this moment. Emmaline wore black workout tights and a stretchy black warm-up jacket, zipped to her chin. Her hair looked freshly blown out. Guy's smile tensed somewhat when he saw Lettie, but he recovered his composure with an ear-to-ear grin.

"Oh Lettie, look what we've gone and done," Emmaline said and held her hand out. She was wearing silver rings on two of her fingers and one on her thumb and Lettie scanned carefully for a diamond. No stone, but the thickest of the silver rings had the word LOVE engraved on it.

"Beautiful rings. What's the occasion?" she asked, heart sinking. Surely, they weren't engaged. Guy was so wrong for her, deceptive and fake.

"Just celebrating the fact that we met," Guy said with a glance at Emmaline. He held out his right hand and she saw a matching silver band engraved with LOVE on his middle finger.

"Our one-month anniversary," Emmaline said.

Guy flung his arm around her like she was his property and pulled her into his chest. "Bad girl," he said in a playful tone. "I ought to give you a swat. You know we met on March 15, so that makes today one month and three days. March 15 was Mrs. Ahern's birthday, and you'd come by to drop off some banana bread from your mom." He lowered his voice then to its most confidential pitch. "Isn't she just so forgetful?"

Lettie didn't bite. This guy acted like there were television cameras recording his every word and a studio audience laughing at his dorky banter. She smiled but it felt self-conscious and false, like the pasted-on smiles people get when posing for too many photos.

"I love Emmaline," she said. "She's like my big sister." It was a dorky thing to say but it was all she could manage with the war going on inside her head after that talk with Angel.

"Of course you do. And I'm falling in love with her too, right, honey?" He squeezed Emmaline again.

"I'm going to bring that Easter dress over for Milly soon," Emmaline said. "I'm just putting the final touches on it tonight."

"It's a beautiful dress," Guy said. "Her hand-stitching is amazing. I've seen couture dresses before, back in California, and I'm here to tell you, this dress could be sold by Gucci or Caroline Herrera for thousands of dollars. Thousands." His tone was suddenly argumentative, as though Lettie had insulted the dress. She could feel red flags waving but couldn't guess what was coming.

"I can't wait to see Milly in it," Lettie said.

Guy held onto Emmaline but leaned into Lettie, wagging a finger at her. "You really ought to pay her for that dress... The amount of time she's spent on it. I told Emmaline and I'll say it to you. It's the least you could do after she's done all this amazing handiwork on it, and you can't even be bothered to drop by to see it."

"What?"

Guy pinned her with the glint of broken ice in his eyes and closed the gap between them as Emmaline tugged on his shirt. "Don't act like you don't know what I mean. Last time we saw you, she asked you to come by to see the dress. She was so excited to show you and you couldn't even make ten minutes of your time available to her. Just like an egocentric teenager. Do you know how much people pay for custom-made dresses like that? You're a selfish, entitled little kid."

"Guy!" Emmaline interrupted. She seemed baffled that he had started this conversation, but it was clearly something they had discussed. "Let's drop this right now. Another time. She's trying to take a walk and I'm sure she could use some time to herself, busy little mama that she is."

"She can spare a few minutes, I'm sure," Guy said with a mean flash in his eyes and a sneer on his lips.

"Sure," Lettie said in a quiet voice. She looked at Emmaline. "Have you been mad at me?" She felt her breath lock in her chest and the trailer park grew close and sharp as she waited for Emmaline's response. Did Em really feel like Lettie didn't appreciate her?

Guy spoke before Emmaline had the chance. "Let's not put Emmaline on the spot," he said. "She adores you which is why she would never bring this up. But someone needs to tell you to wake up and smell the coffee already. How could you take her for granted like that? You're lucky to have her."

"I don't take Emmaline for granted."

"Sure looks like it to me," Guy said. "I don't want to call you a liar but—"

Lettie felt her jaw drop, and her mind couldn't find words to respond. She was the sixteen-year-old mother of a baby, consumed with caring for her infant daughter, trying to stay in high school and hold her family together. Maybe she was selfish, not just with Emmaline, but also with Angel. Maybe she did only think about herself and the baby. That was all she had energy for some days.

"We can talk about this later," Emmaline said, grabbing Guy by the wrist and tugging him away. Even as he moved toward her, he kept his ice eyes on Lettie, his face painted in angry red splotches.

As Lettie continued to the mailroom, she felt her heart thumping and realized she was damp with sweat. She opened the door and collapsed against the wall of mailboxes, crying once again.

When Lettie arrived home, it was late afternoon, and the mobile home was quiet and dark. Ballpoint padded out of Verda's room to meet her, pushing his nose under her hand in search of a pat, which she readily gave the pit bull. The kitchen was tidy, the television turned off, and the room she shared with Angel and Milly was empty. Angel must have gone back to Atomic Video Games and Zane still at work. Verda's bedroom door was half-shut but she could hear soft voices emanating from the room. Lettie listened at the door for a moment to make sure Verda wasn't in there with Leon.

"Shh, shh, little one, back to sleep," Verda said. "Hush now." Milly protested the start of a cry that could fade to whimper or ascend to howl. Lettie pushed the door open to find her grandmother on the bed next to Milly, who worked her arms and legs like she was crawling on air.

Verda's bedroom was grandmotherly with floral wallpaper and dark furniture, black-and-white photos of her and her late husband Osbert and Lettie's mom, Lily, in tiny metal frames, a curio cabinet full of crystal figurines. A stack of light grey storage bins lined the walls and made the room feel claustrophobic.

"What happened?" Verda said when she saw Lettie's face.

"I had an encounter with Emmaline's new boyfriend," she replied.

"Hmm," Verda said.

Lettie leaned over to plant a kiss on Milly's fat cheek, but Milly was only interested in her own feet. Her latest favorite trick was putting her toes in her mouth. The adorableness took the edge off Lettie's anxiety. Lettie was in love with the activity and with her tiny perfect feet.

Verda stroked Milly's forehead. "I met that fellow. He seems like a jerk."

"Grandma, he's nuts. He's accusing me of taking advantage of Emmaline by not paying for that Easter dress she's been sewing for Milly. I didn't ask Emmaline to make that. She volunteered!"

Milly made a little sighing sound and Lettie felt her milk let down. Soon the baby would start crying with hunger, Lettie could sense it. Her breasts engorged as though full of rocks and the front of her shirt got wet. Lettie reached over to pick Milly off the bed, and the baby reached for the front of Lettie's sweatshirt. Milly played with strands of Lettie's hair as she nursed, eyes wide open.

Verda crossed to the dresser and grabbed her phone.

"You're not calling Emmaline, are you?" Lettie asked with alarm.

"Hush." Verda held a hand up as a woman's voice said hello through the speaker.

"Hello, dear. This is Verda Davis. What are you doing right now?"

"I was just getting ready to sit in the sun a bit. You know, get my vitamin D. Do you want to come over and sit with me?" Lettie recognized the voice of Mrs. Ahern.

"Uh-uh. Not right now. I think you should come over here to talk to me and Lettie about something. We have a little concern."

Mrs. Ahern agreed and a few minutes later she sat at the kitchen table across from Verda, Lettie, and Milly. She was a large woman, as tall as Zane, with dark brown hair to her shoulders and frizzy bangs. She wore frameless glasses that magnified her eyes, capri jeans, and a Dallas Cowboys T-shirt. She was about the same age as Verda, most famous at the Majestic for leaving her outdoor Christmas decorations up all year because it was easier than the ritual of putting them up and taking them down.

Verda skipped the small talk and launched right in. "Who is this Guy Callahan?" She tapped her fingers on the dining table.

Mrs. Ahern's voice was hesitant and soft. "I don't really know. He came to my door one day, said he saw an ad on Craig's List about a rental. But it was a mix-up of some kind. I wasn't renting any rooms and I told him that. He looked just as pathetic as a lost dog and it was raining, I remember that. He said he had nowhere to go, so I invited him in just to get dry for a minute and check his phone to see if he'd gotten the address wrong. He hadn't gotten it wrong though. He showed me the email and everything. Someone had made an ad on one of those websites that I was renting a room out. He said there were lots of scammers out there and this wasn't the first time he'd been tricked. He said the worst of it was that he'd sent this scammer two hundred and fifty dollars as a security deposit already, so he was probably out of that money."

"So, you decided to take him in?" Verda stared at Mrs. Ahern skeptically.

Mrs. Ahern seemed to shrink into the chair under Verda's gaze. "I just said he could stay with me until he found a place. He insisted on paying rent."

"Where's he from?" Lettie asked. Milly finished nursing and wiped her face on Lettie's sweatshirt then plunked her head down on her mother's shoulder.

Mrs. Ahern crossed and then uncrossed her arms and legs, fidgeting so much that the expression "ants in her pants" popped into Lettie's brain and wouldn't leave.

"Um—California, I think."

"Where in California?"

"San Francisco, maybe?"

"You let this strange man move into your home and you don't know where he is from?" Verda said. "Sweetie, what were you thinking?"

"I don't know. He seemed like a nice young man. I wanted to help him, and I thought it wasn't the worst idea to have a man living in the house, you know, for protection." Mrs. Ahern let out a quick, high-pitched laugh but Lettie didn't think it sounded funny at all. In fact, it sounded downright strange.

"Do you think maybe you could find out where he is from exactly?" Lettie said. "There's something weird about him. And he told me he was from lots of places but mentioned San Diego specifically. Maybe Zane can investigate, make sure everything is on the up-and-up."

Now Mrs. Ahern's eyes grew even wider behind her frameless glasses. "Do you think I'm in danger? What have I done? He's a very private person. He's made it clear he doesn't like me asking a lot of questions."

"Maybe you can find out more about him in a way he doesn't have to know about," Lettie said. "When he's gone, go in his room and look around a bit. I think it might be important not to let him know we're looking for more information about him."

Mrs. Ahern looked trapped. Her internal debate was plastered all over her face. Should she risk getting caught spying on Guy or be potentially blindsided by a scam he was trying to run on her? It was going to be a close contest, but Lettie was confident Mrs. Ahern would side with them.

As their neighbor left, Lettie thought of all she had to do in the early evening: the nightly rituals of bath time and clothing changes and more nursing, all the lifting and bending and rocking. Angel had texted he wouldn't be home tonight until after eight so that meant it was all on her. Just like it would be if he were to move to Oklahoma City even if she were to follow him. Days and days of nursing, diaper changes, and nap schedules, all those tiny decisions about pacifier use and letting Milly cry versus picking her up. It was exhausting. She wanted to crawl under the dining table and cry. And yet she still needed to rally enough to walk over to the Perrymans' and see the dress Emmaline was making for Milly and find the energy to look excited. She was grateful for the dress, she truly was. But she had no idea where she could summon the strength to do the basics, let alone the extras. She knew she had to, though. Emmaline was too important to her to not follow through. Maybe tomorrow.

Chapter 18
Zane

Tuesday morning, Tulsa was dim and sluggish as Zane headed into the office from his sleepover bodyguard duties at Tiffany's. He felt frazzled but amped up. They were close to a break in the case with Tyler Swinton and it seemed like they were getting results faster than the police. Loris had called a friend and fellow detective named Robert Kaplan in Dallas to look into Tyler Swinton. According to Loris' text, Kaplan had talked his way into Swinton's office this morning and turned around a quick report.

Kaplan was already on the video call when Zane walked into the office. The camera angle he had chosen was unfortunate. Zane and Loris had a clear shot up his nostrils as he talked about turkey hunting in north Texas. He wore a yellow polo shirt bright enough to be a hunter's safety vest and the color glowed like the sun against his dark brown skin.

"People say just get out and start hunting, but a 250-pound Black man like me has to be careful driving around rural Texas with a rifle in the back of his truck and hiking into public spaces around other gun-toting folk. So, I've got this farmer friend who lets me hunt on his land and that works out best for me.”

“You oughta come up north and hunt on my Uncle Brian’s land. He sees deer, elk, and antelope in the winter.”

“Count on it,” Kaplan said.

“Hey, here’s Zane now.”

Zane pulled a chair up next to Loris at her desk and said hi and nice to meet you and all that. After they exchanged the niceties, Kaplan got down to business.

“Nothing too much to report really,” he said. “It always helps me to see a subject with my own eyes instead of just photos on a computer screen. He’s a middle-aged slouch who might have been a better version of himself twenty-two years ago. The office isn’t much. It was two rooms—him in one and another guy with body odor behind three computer screens in the other. I told him I was with the property management company, and we were taking a survey to decide whether to bring food trucks to the parking lot for lunch once a month. He couldn’t have cared less about that. Said he brought his lunch because he was on some keto diet or something. I asked him about his business as much as I could without him getting too suspicious. I thought of asking him if he took cryptocurrency because you said that was part of the case, but that might have raised a red flag or two. I had been thinking on my way to his office that I’d try to lift something that would have his fingerprints on it, but he was watching me the whole time. If he and his friend leave, the door would be no problem. Standard lock. I could open it easy.”

“Good to know,” Loris said. “Did you see any obvious connections between this company and WorthComm?”

Kaplan shook his head. “No blinking signs or anything. I tried to probe a bit into his background, but he wasn’t having any of it and I didn’t want to push too hard.”

"I appreciate it," Loris said. "Can I pay you for your time?"

"Naw, not necessary. But I'll let you know if you can return the favor. You never know."

Loris disconnected the call after they exchanged the usual goodbye pleasantries. "A lot of PIs won't take money for helping out another PI. They'd rather have the favor. And don't doubt it—I'm sure he'll be asking for one. It's just how it works."

It made sense to Zane. He was about the spend the afternoon running down Tyler Swinton's connections to WorthComm in 2001 and the best place to start was going to be with Derrick. So far, he'd been relying on her desire to spill the tea on anything and everything WorthComm, but he wasn't sure when that motivation was going to need supplementing, though he had no idea what else would get her talking.

While he waited for Derrick to respond, he frittered away two hours looking at emails and messages from the ads and other inquiries he had made. Out of fifty-five emails and messages, only three were promising. The first one was from a man who worked the cash registers at the WorthComm cafeteria for fifteen years, which meant he had only started in 2007. But he knew someone who had worked there before him, and he had an email for her. Her name was Bertha Gonzales, and Zane sent her an email and spent some time trying to find a phone number for her too without much luck.

More waiting. Detective work like this resulted in a lot of dead ends. With evidence now that Tyler Swinton linked not just to WorthComm but also to Sherwood Rittenhour directly, Zane scoured every email with leads or suggestions. The second email that looked promising was from someone who said she was a product engineer back then. She didn't know Diana Granger but knew another person who did a lot of work in the executive offices back then. That person turned out to be Derrick, so Zane thanked the woman for her time but had to break the news that there would be no reward for information they already had. Though it was nice to have independent confirmation about Derrick's knowledge and presence at WorthComm back in the day.

The third email that got his attention was from a woman named Heather Guilder who had worked as an assistant in human resources for WorthComm back in the early 2000s. She had been the person responsible for exit interviews. Zane hadn't heard the term "exit interview" before but got the gist quickly: Heather had been the person who filled out the paperwork when employees left WorthComm. She remembered Diana Granger's exit interview because she got a call from Sherwood Rittenhour about it, asking to know what reason Diana had given for leaving. It wasn't too often that an HR assistant talked to the CEO on the phone, and it was notable because he was the one who called her directly, not his assistant. The call had lasted only a few minutes, but Heather remembered asking her supervisor if she knew of a connection between them. Her boss told her to mind her own business. Anyway, Diana Granger had just said she had another job opportunity more in line with her interests in IT.

Zane decided to press his luck with Heather, asking her via email if she had heard of Tyler Swinton but she hadn't. She did have another lead for him, remembering that a woman who worked in recruiting back then had been dating someone who worked in business development and maybe she would know Tyler Swinton. Zane was starting to feel like he was chasing his tail, but he addressed one more email to Jennette Felton.

The response from Jennette came fast. She suggested a call and went so far as to say that she was free right then if he could talk, so Zane took her up on the offer. A few minutes later, they were looking at each other through computer screens, this time on some video conferencing software called BlueJeans that

Zane had to download. Was there no end to the number of companies offering video conferencing these days?

Jennette Felton was about fifty with silver hair that grazed her shoulders and blue eyes that were as quick and alert as a fox's. She was busy. The thirty minutes Zane spent on the call with her would have been maybe ten if her phone and email hadn't interrupted her several times.

"What can I tell you about WorthComm? I loved that place. Miss it every day. I work for myself now which is great, but I loved that team at WorthComm. We felt like we were doing something special then."

"I don't know what you can tell me, Ms. Felton, but I've got some questions for you. I work for a private investigator named Loris Trapper in Tulsa and we're working on a job that has some roots going back twenty-two years. So, it's the year 2001 I'm interested in. What were you doing at WorthComm back then?"

"I was on the people solutions team back then. I was in talent acquisitions which basically meant recruiting new employees."

"Heather Guilder said you dated someone in business development back then."

"She has an amazing memory. I'd forgotten all about that little tryst. I used to have to go to these community events and staff booths. You know the kind of thing: handing out brochures, encouraging people to check out our job listings. For some of them I got paired up with someone from business development. Good old Max Duron. We went out a couple of times."

"Did you know Tyler Swinton? He also worked in business development then."

"I wouldn't say I knew him well, but yes, I knew him. He worked the booths with me and Max at the Dallas Regional

Chamber's Annual Meeting and some others. We talked about WorthComm, the weather, that kind of thing."

"Can I share my screen? I want to show you a photo," Zane said. She agreed, but the BlueJeans interface perplexed Zane so much that he wound up holding his phone up to the computer's camera.

Jennette leaned into the screen, squinting for a moment. Her phone went off like a siren and she turned away for a few moments to tell someone what to do and then hung up. "Show me again," she said in the manner of someone used to people obeying her commands, and he complied. After a few beats, her eyes widened and looked at him. "Diana something, right? That's Diana Granger. That's who Heather said you were interested in initially. I thought I saw an ad or something about it last week."

"You knew her?"

"Yes. She worked with Tyler on some project. I don't remember what it was about, but I remember being in some meeting about community partnerships and who we were going to give sponsorship money to, and she was there with Tyler."

Zane had dual and conflicting urges right then. First, he wanted to leap through the computer and give her a big hug. Second, he wanted to shake her for not answering the ad a week ago. He only acted on the first urge. "Ms. Felton, you have literally made my day. And I'm personally going to see to it that we get you some of that reward money from our client."

She smiled but shook her head. "I didn't do much really, just told you a fact from the deep folds of my memory. But apparently, I've uncovered some kind of needle in a haystack for you."

"That's exactly it. You've helped us make a connection we weren't sure we were going to make."

"So, is Diana Granger your client? No, that doesn't make sense, does it? Why would you have placed that ad if she were."

"No, Diana is dead. She adopted a new name, Dawn Renee, and someone murdered her. I would tell you about it, but you're busy and our client wants to keep certain facts confidential as much as possible. Can I ask you a few more questions?"

Her phone's siren ring tone shrieked again. This time it took longer because she was telling someone what not to do. She finally finished it and returned her attention to Zane. "Can I ask you a question first? I liked Diana. She impressed me as a very competent young woman. I didn't see a lot of her, but we did have lunch once or twice. I was trying to recruit her for a position on my team in HR. She was hard-working and smart, but she had come in working for Sherwood on some special project and then wound up in business development, but her interest was in IT and computers. She wanted to do nerd stuff, not people stuff as she put it. You said she's dead. Would she want you to be making these inquiries?"

Zane lied. He could have dodged and wriggled, said a bunch of nonsense about how he didn't know her and couldn't possibly guess, but he knew certainty was called for, so he gave it. "Yes," he said. "She would approve. It was a long time ago, but you may remember. When did you first see her with Tyler Swinton?"

"I think it was winter 2001. My divorce was final in December 2000, Merry Christmas to me, and I was volunteering to take on assignments where I could meet people. I was on the rebound hard. I remember being in some meetings around that time with Diana."

"Do you remember when you saw her last?"

"Not definitely but I remember noticing she wasn't around, and I asked Tyler and Max about her. They just gave me some vague answer about her wanting to work in IT. So that's what I assume she did, though not for WorthComm."

"Was that in the spring, summer, or fall?"

"Not the fall. Not that long after. By April or something, I think, because a specialist on our team in HR had left, and I wanted to see if Diana was interested in the job, but she was gone."

"Didn't you work in HR? I would figure you'd know who came and went."

"It was a big company. I didn't even work in the same area as the people who did the employee separations. The only way her leaving might have crossed my desk is if they posted her position for recruitment, and now that I think about it, they never did. She got that position as a special transfer originated by the CEO, and when she left, they didn't refill it."

"Was that common?"

"I wouldn't say it was common, but it happens. Privilege of power and all that. Middle managers and run-of-the-mill vice presidents must jump through lots of hoops to hire. They ask for the budget, justify the job, go through a big recruiting process with job postings and an objective evaluation panel. CEO-types like Sherwood Rittenhour just send an email that says, 'find this person a job' and that's the extent of the process."

"Would you say that she worked with Tyler Swinton on a daily basis?"

"I would imagine so. I didn't have insight into their day-to-day other than what I heard from Max. Max didn't think much of Tyler. Said he was lazy. Also, Tyler had one of those CEO-directed jobs too. He didn't get the job through typical recruitment from what I heard. But Max didn't have the details really and it's all kind of fuzzy now. I just remember the impression that Tyler had connections somehow."

"Did you like him?"

"Nope, not really. Like I said, I didn't know him, but I didn't want to get to know him any better from what I saw. He thought he was handsome and charming, and I'll admit, he had an appeal. But he was too slick for me. The kind of man who doesn't just shake hands but who clasps both hands around yours and squeezes, telling you how delighted he is to meet you. Big eye contact and all that. Reminded me of a sleazy politician. Not the kind of man I wanted to work with or date. Don't tell me Tyler Swinton is your client."

"No, he is not. Tell me, what did Diana think of Tyler? Did you ever talk about him with her?"

Her phone rang again—an important client, judging by the conversation—and then she stabbed a couple of quick texts into her phone and sighed. "It's a cliché but it's hard to find good problem solvers these days. You looking for work? I could use a smart young man like you."

"I appreciate the offer but I'm trying to get into this private investigator field. I like the work and getting to meet interesting people like you."

"HR has some of that, but maybe not as much as you'd like. But you call me anytime if you're looking to make a change, Zane. And about your other question. I think Diana might have been a bit snowed by Tyler. He was a heavy-duty player. But she was younger than me so maybe she hadn't seen the signs before. Like I said, he had a charm, and I won't deny he was good-looking. I'm sure she could tell my opinion was a little less than favorable so maybe that's why we never talked about him. At least not that I can remember. She was very much her own person."

"Do you have a PayPal or Venmo so I can get some of that reward money to you?"

"No. I mean, it's not necessary. I liked Diana, and if you say this is helping her then that's enough for me."

There weren't many people who would turn down reward money. Jennette Fulton was a real friend to Diana Granger. Zane felt guilty about lying that Diana would have approved of the work he and Loris were doing. But if Jennette's information led to the identity of Diana's killer, certainly the lie would be justified. If there was one thing Zane had learned, it was that private investigators had to lie sometimes to get information, despite being in the business of uncovering the truth.

Chapter 19
Zane

When Loris returned from the courthouse on Tuesday afternoon, Zane was all business. "I'll skip the painful hours of dead-end rabbit holes and reading countless irrelevant emails. A woman named Jennette Fulton who used to work in human resources at WorthComm back in the early 2000s knew both Tyler Swinton and Diana Granger and can put them together in early 2001."

Loris set her black nylon backpack on the desk and turned to face him. "So, it's possible that when Dawn ran out of that restaurant, she could have been running from Tyler just as easily as Sherwood."

"It still doesn't add up. Here's what we know. Diana Granger worked closely with Tyler Swinton in the early months of 2001. Both received special consideration for jobs in the WorthComm business development office due to their connections to Sherwood Rittenhour. Diana got pregnant around March 2001 and gave birth to our client, Kayla Renee, on December 4, 2001. Fast forward twenty-some years. Pickert forces her to take a trip to Fort Worth for work, and she runs into Sherwood Rittenhour and Tyler Swinton. A month later, she's been poisoned, and her daughter finds a hard wallet containing a million dollars in cryptocurrency."

"And the clincher," Loris said, "is this: Tyler Swinton came to see Diana aka Dawn at the Pickert Real Estate offices a few days before she died, and he was angry. I think Pastor would be mad if we held all those things back at this point. But what's the connection between Sherwood Rittenhour and Tyler Swinton? Are they related?" Loris narrowed her eyes and Zane was pretty sure she was thinking what he was thinking. Tyler could be Rittenhour's dirty little secret, a hidden son. It was starting to fall into place, but they needed real evidence, not just speculation.

Zane shook his head. "If there's a connection it's a well-kept secret which is kind of amazing these days. I've found nothing online or through Derrick or any of the other WorthComm sources we've found. The DNA test showed a relationship to Curtis Rittenhour—could also be an uncle, a sibling—it's just guesswork without some more testing. The police are doing that."

Loris slid into her seat and leaned back. "If Swinton's the father but not the murderer, the DNA test is key, and our approach might be a direct one," she said. "It also casts a less sinister light on his overture to Kayla Renee at the Boot Barn. It is possible he just wants to know his daughter and had a clunky approach with that job offer. If that is the case, then he may agree to submit to a DNA test quite easily. If he is the father *and* the murderer, the situation is simpler. He killed Dawn and maybe her boyfriend too."

"And he could be a threat to Kayla." Zane reflexively grabbed his phone and stared blankly at its dark screen. "Do we trick him into coming to talk to us, like we did with Sherwood Rittenhour?"

"He has already reached out to Kayla directly, so maybe that's our path forward. We just need to keep her safe and I don't want to expose her to him. It might get ugly."

"Roger that," Zane said. "I think I can imitate a twenty-two-year-old woman in texts. I have had some experience with them."

He and Loris hashed out the plan they would execute on Wednesday, and Zane headed home.

Lettie, Ballpoint, and Verda pounced on him as he entered the mobile home in a chaotic welcome and information dump. He blinked to try to keep up with all the sensory details coming at him: Ballpoint's rough tongue licking his hand, the smell of tomato sauce and chicken cooking, and Lettie and Verda asking him about what he thought of Emmaline's new boyfriend.

"Slow down, slow down," Zane said, walking to the couch with Ballpoint bumping against his thigh as the dog kept pace with every step.

"There's something off with this guy... who is named Guy." Lettie followed him to the couch but continued to stand, hands on her hips and reminding him of their mother. "It's suspicious if you ask me. He just showed up at Mrs. Ahern's with a weird story about an ad to rent a room from her."

"And he's been saying Lettie should pay Emmaline for that Easter dress she's making for Milly," Verda said. "That doesn't sound like Emmaline."

"She's had bad taste in men for years," Zane said. "Why would that change now?"

"Agreed but this one seems worse than usual," Lettie said. "Like he's got some scam going or something. He seems dishonest. And you know Emmaline has been making some money lately from the Instagram creators' fund. Her videos and stuff are taking off. Not quite rent money, she told me, but enough to cover her expenses lately. So maybe this guy is an opportunist."

Those were strong words from Lettie. Zane's guardian radar pinged. He had been in love with Emmaline for years, starting when they were kids and lasting into his twenties before she broke the spell by telling him she'd never love him back. He still felt protective of her, despite the now-healed broken heart.

"What do you want me to do about it?"

"Come with me to Emmaline's to see the dress tonight. Talk to her. I bet he'll be there. He doesn't leave her side these days. It's kind of creepy."

"Emmaline is a beautiful woman. People naturally want to be around her," Zane said.

"You'll see," Lettie said.

"Fine, I'll come with you," Zane said. "But I don't want to stay long."

The front door of the Perrymans' mobile home was open, and the smoky smell of beef and spices wafted through the screen. Zane peered in and spotted Emmaline in the kitchen with her mother, washing and drying dishes at the sink.

"Hello!"

The two women turned. "Well, Zane and Lettie. What a nice surprise," Glynnis Perryman said. She came over and unlatched the screen then held the door open for them. She was wearing a lavender caftan, the wide sleeves decorated with floral embroidery in a darker shade of violet. A small barrette in the shape of a butterfly adorned her short grey hair. She seemed relaxed and happy to see them. "Come in, come in. Would you like some brisket? We just put it away, but I can make you a plate."

They declined the offer but still followed her into the oblong kitchen—oak cabinets, faux granite countertops covered in green houseplants, and one long window looking out onto a thick power line swaying in the light wind outside. Lettie entered hesitantly, as though expecting Guy Callahan to jump out of a cabinet.

Emmaline finished drying a dish and put it in the cabinet, her silky blonde ponytail swishing across the back of her pink hoodie. "They came to see Milly's Easter dress." She turned to face them, and Zane was startled by her eyes, which had changed from their usual brown to a bold green framed by thick, dark lashes. It was a trick of cosmetics, probably achieved for some paid sponsorship video: colored contact lenses and false eyelashes. With her narrow face and pointed chin, the overall effect was elfen-like and ethereal. Together, Emmaline and her mother looked like an illustration from a fairy tale, delicate and beautiful and other-worldly.

"Green-eyed lady," Zane said, feeling a goofy grin come over him. What was it about Emmaline that always affected him so? He was in love with Tiffany and knew he had no chance with Em, but his childhood crush seemed to defy time and logic. Tiffany was always jealous of Emmaline, and this was probably why. His old feelings for her surfaced far too often.

"I remember that song," Glynnis said. "I'm surprised you know an oldie like that." She began to sing the song in a melancholy fashion.

"We don't want to interrupt anything," Lettie said. "Is Guy here?"

"No, not right now," Emmaline said. "He had some business to take care of, but he should be back around eight or so. We're going to sing karaoke tonight. Maybe I'll do this Green-Eyed Lady song. Guy would like that. The contacts were his idea."

"Fun," Zane said automatically. He and Lettie followed

Emmaline into her sewing room, a rectangular space dominated by a gigantic, L-shaped workstation made of two pine tables. The longer one was her main workstation, cluttered with a blue plastic cutting board, glass containers filled with buttons sorted by color, a tan basket filled with bobbins, bottles of fabric paint, and two red-checked pin cushions.

The smaller table held Emmaline's white sewing machine, a Brother model her parents had bought her for her high school graduation. Scissors, a measuring tape, and pink, purple, and blue fabric swatches hung from a corkboard on the wall behind the sewing machine. Next to them were photos of her pageant clients dressed in her creations. Milly's Easter dress, impossibly small and a confection of pink and yellow ruffles with floral trim, hung from a tiny hanger on a hook by the door.

"It's beautiful," Lettie said, touching the ruffles and surprised by their softness. "She'll be the best-dressed girl in Tulsa. You've outdone yourself."

Emmaline's face brightened and she ran her fingers along the dress hem. "You like it? The floral trim was Guy's idea. I tell you, he is so creative. He gives me so many great ideas."

"That's awesome," Lettie said. She wrapped her arms around Emmaline and gave her a squeeze. "Thank you again."

"It's really something special, Em," Zane said.

"Thank you!" Emmaline pulled away from Lettie to face Zane. "And Zane, I want you to get to know Guy better. You're going to really like him once you do, I think. He makes me feel unstoppable. Just like how I think Tiffany makes you feel. Like there are no obstacles."

Zane and Lettie exchanged glances. Was Emmaline going to pass right over Guy's insisting that they pay for the Easter dress?

"I thought maybe you'd bring Milly over to try it on, but we can do that another time," Emmaline said.

"She's down for the night." Lettie shifted uncomfortably from foot to foot. "I thought maybe you and I should have a talk after Guy's comments about the cost of the dress."

Emmaline waved her concern away. "Don't worry about that. He was just in a mood. Hashtag grumpy if you know what I mean."

"But Emmaline, I don't want you to feel like I'm taking advantage of you. Shouldn't we talk about it?"

"No. I don't think you're taking advantage of me."

Lettie was skeptical. "But Guy does."

"No, that's not it. You got the wrong idea from him."

Lettie felt her eyebrows fly high. Guy's communication had been clear as a bell. "The wrong idea?"

"It's really my fault. I should have straightened it out at the time. Guy overreacted and he realizes that. In fact, he wants to make it up to you. We had a long talk about it afterwards and I know he felt terrible. It had nothing to do with you personally. He gets triggered when he thinks someone is taking advantage. It goes way back to his childhood. He's a really good person. If you spend some time with him, you'll see what I mean."

"I hope so," Zane said. "From what Lettie said, he said some harsh things. I wasn't sure what was going on."

Emmaline gave a pretty tinkling laugh. "He's all bark and no bite. Like Ballpoint. I wouldn't take it too seriously. Guy's the real deal. And he's just as loyal as Ballpoint too."

"I just don't want to see you get caught up in something weird." Zane wasn't a hundred percent sure what he meant by "something weird" but it seemed to fit.

"I know, I know. I don't have a great record with boyfriends lately." Emmaline picked up a red pincushion and tossed it from hand to hand. "But Guy treats me like a lady. You don't need to worry about me and Guy. I've got it under control." She glanced at Zane. "I've been talking to him about becoming my manager. He has great ideas about how I can get more product sponsorships. He thinks I can make a living as a content creator in the sewing and beauty online spaces."

"Oh really?"

"That's how the whole idea of charging for the dress even came up. I was telling him how long it takes me to sew a dress and he crunched the numbers to figure out my hourly rate and let me tell you... That really opened my eyes. He thinks I should charge more money for the dresses in general. But I explained to him that y'all are basically family and that I offered to make the dress. He understood that. He didn't mean to interfere in our relationship. He was just looking out for me."

Zane noticed that Emmaline was speed-talking and bouncing from foot to foot, a sure sign she was over-excited and not thinking too clearly. So, he decided to get into the specifics with her. "What would being your manager mean, exactly?"

Emmaline giggled. "Helping me book gigs and get sponsorships. Introducing me around to the different PR firms and stuff. Helping me manage my money coming in and developing some paid advertising too to help spread the word about the pageant gown business."

"PR firms here in Tulsa?" Zane tried to keep his face neutral as he asked the question. This sounded shady.

"Well, around the country really. He has a lot of connections in California so maybe another trip out west. He swore me to secrecy but some of the people he knows would amaze you. Top people at some of the big tech companies and they know all the brands."

Make that *super* shady, Zane thought.

"You're going back to Los Angeles?" Lettie interjected.

"Not me. Guy would go ahead of me and lay the groundwork. I'd come out later. I don't understand all the details, but he knows what he's doing. He used to work for Facebook and

Snapchat. Made a ton of money in stock options from some start-up. He thought he had retired at the ripe old age of twenty-five, but I've got him thinking about getting back into the business."

"Huh," Zane said. "If he's got a bunch of money, why is he renting a room from Mrs. Ahern at the Majestic?"

"His money's tied up. He can't liquidate it, so he lives simply. He likes it that way. He wanted to check out Tulsa because he'd read so much about how it's becoming a creative hub. Like Paris in the 1930s or something, with the Bob Dylan Center and the Woody Guthrie Center and the reconciliation work being done in Historic Greenwood. He's talking about buying a house here just as soon as he sells his in Northern California."

It sounded like pure babble to Zane but before he could ask any more questions, he heard the door open, and a male voice say hello to Glynnis.

"Here he is now," Emmaline said.

Zane darted a look at Lettie, who was grimacing at the floor. He reached over to squeeze her arm in a show of solidarity. No one was going to bully his little sister while he was around.

Guy appeared in the doorway, and when he saw Lettie, he shook his head sheepishly and cupped his hand over his mouth. His shoulders curved over his chest, giving him a sunken appearance. "Oh Lettie. Here you are. I'm sure I know why you're here." He stepped fully into the room and paused for a moment, hands steepled in front of his chest as though praying. "Let me talk first before you say one word." He looked at Emmaline. "Oh Em, you told her I didn't mean all that stuff I said about the dress, didn't you?" His voice was beseeching and high-pitched and it grated on Zane.

But Emmaline went to his side and grabbed his hand for a

reassuring squeeze. "I've explained and I know they under-stand. No worries."

"I wish I could turn the worry switch off just like that, hedgehog, but it doesn't work that way. I better just make my own apologies."

Hedgehog? Zane and Lettie leaned into one another, trying not to laugh.

Guy stepped toward Lettie and took her hand, pressing it between his own.

"I'm so sorry. I butted into something that was none of my business and I am deeply apologetic." His tone was remorseful and pleading. "What do you think? Ten lashes with a wet noodle as punishment?"

Lettie extricated her hand from his grip and stepped back-wards. "Like Emmaline said, no worries here. Let's forget all about it."

Guy's eyes skipped over Lettie to Zane and for a moment, Zane saw cold calculation in his eyes before it vanished into over-the-top remorse. Guy extended his right hand to Zane for a shake. "Friends?"

Just to show him he was no fool, Zane took his hand and gave it a harder squeeze than necessary, which Guy matched in intensity for a few moments as they locked eyes with fake smiles inked on their faces. Guy pulled back first with a smarmy grin and laugh. Hedgehog laughed too, seeming pleased that everyone was friends. With a few more compli-ments about the dress and Emmaline's handiwork, Lettie and Zane made their excuses to leave. Guy was too busy fussing with his smartphone suddenly to pay too much attention to them as they departed.

"I couldn't wait to get out of there," Lettie said as they walked home. "I needed to be away from the grinning face of that guy named Guy."

"And I'm starving," Zane said. "There is definitely something off with Guy. I think I'm going to take this investigation to the next level."

"What does that mean?"

"You don't need to know, Lettie."

"Now you've got to tell me."

Zane slapped at his arm as he felt the sting of a mosquito bite. "I want to go check out his room at Mrs. Ahern's."

"I want to come!" Lettie grabbed at his arm and squeezed. A screen door slammed somewhere in the distance.

"One of us breaking the law is enough," Zane said. He was supposed to be the voice of reason but Lettie's interest in going was hard to refuse. He always had a hard time saying no to her, even when he should. It only took a few more pleases before he gave in and said she could come. If he were honest, he wanted to show her a little bit about his new skills as a private investigator.

Lettie and Zane returned home and dined on Verda's delicious chicken stew full of tomatoes, onions, and peppers. Zane kept getting up from the table to look through the living room window blinds to see if Emmaline and Guy had left yet for the karaoke bar. Finally, around seven forty-five, he saw Emmaline's car drive toward the exit.

He finished dinner and grabbed the private investigator's kit Loris had given him containing master keys, key picks, a small knife, and a flashlight, and he and Lettie headed to Mrs. Ahern's front door. The older woman cracked open the door still festooned with a faded Christmas wreath and peered at them with her eyebrows squished together. She opened the door with a frown. "I wasn't expecting anyone at this hour." As though eight o'clock on a Tuesday evening was midnight.

Lettie and Zane probably hadn't visited Mrs. Ahern since Lettie was young enough to trick or treat on Halloween, and her pursed lips and glances over his shoulder let him know that she suspected they were here to snoop on her roommate. Still, she held the door open wide for them to enter and forced a smile. The television was on and a commercial about male health supplements touted increased virility.

"I thought I'd do a little background check on your tenant," Zane said, as the commercial gave way to a blonde news anchor in high outrage about something that happened on Twitter.

"He's not here right now." Mrs. Ahern started biting her lip and took a few steps to block Zane and Lettie from entering the short hallway leading to two bedrooms and a bathroom.

Zane sidestepped around her, and Lettie followed. "Is his room on the left?" It was the only closed door.

Mrs. Ahern plodded after them, her steps heavy on the mobile home's squeaky foundation. Her facial expression was pinched and worried.

Lettie tried the doorknob. "Locked," she said with a shake of her head.

"You can't go in there."

Lettie set her jaw and anchored her gaze on the older woman. "Mrs. Ahern, you know something is off with him. And tonight, we heard how he's trying to start managing Emmaline's money and going into some partnership."

"I don't know anything about that."

Zane could hear Mrs. Ahern breathing fast behind him as he tried the first master key in the keyhole. The lock was a simple one, easy to open with one of several skeleton keys. He just had to find the right one.

"He locked that door." Mrs. Ahern's voice was shaky and high-pitched, and Zane hoped she wasn't having a panic attack or something.

"Doesn't seem locked to me," Zane said as the second skeleton key turned. He opened the door and Mrs. Ahern stepped backward, her mouth hanging open but no words coming out.

"He's going to be so mad," she finally said.

Zane tried to reassure her. "We're going to be careful as mice. He'll never know we were here. Can you just sit in the living room and let us know if he comes back early for any reason?"

"I'm not a good liar," she said.

Lettie patted her on the back just like she did for Milly when the baby was fussy. "You don't have to lie. Just don't offer any information. Did you ask him where in California he was from?"

"He told me it was a town called Concord in Northern California."

"Did he ever mention anything about working for Facebook or Snapchat?"

"Snap-what? No, I don't think so."

Zane gestured for Lettie to enter the room before him. "We won't be long," he told Mrs. Ahern before closing the bedroom door as she stood there shaking her head. "Be careful, Lettie. He may have laid some traps, like putting pieces of paper along the edges of dresser drawers or stringing dental floss across the top, which if moved would indicate someone had been snooping. Go slow."

At first glance, it appeared Guy had left few traces: no clutter other than a few crumpled coffee receipts on the dresser top, the bedcovers taut. The bedroom was furnished with a mid-century dark wood bedroom set including a four-poster full-size bed so high that Lettie's feet would dangle above the floor if she sat on the edge. The pieces looked like they were real wood, not veneer, the kind of furniture bought at a nice department store and not the secondhand shops where Zane and Lettie found their furnishings. There was a long dresser with a mirror and two matching nightstands flanking the bed with its white chenille bedspread and fuzzy pattern of scrolls and flourishes. Gold-edged frames containing small oil paintings of flowers in vases adorned the pale-yellow walls. A black-and-white photo of a young man in a soldier's uniform had been colorized to add pink to his cheeks and lips and green tones to his cap and jacket. Zane imagined this must be Mr. Ahern in his twenties. Mrs. Ahern had been a widow ever since Zane could remember and the photo of him in his prime washed Zane in sadness.

One wall had a window with drawn white cotton curtains. Zane peeked through the torn window screen to see a tiny patch of winter-white grass punctuated by three stepping stones ending at two metal trash cans and a charcoal grill. If Guy did come back suddenly, they might be able to make an escape through the window, but it would leave too many questions about how the window got open. Plus, he wasn't sure Lettie could handle the leap down since the mobile home's foundation sat about two feet off the ground. Anyway, he was sure that they had one hour at the very least. He'd gone to a karaoke bar with Emmaline before and knew she wouldn't leave until she had a chance to sing at least one song. He went back to the bedroom door and opened it. Mrs. Ahern had turned the television off and was standing at the front window staring out, her body rigid with anxiety. He knew how she felt. His limbs tingled so intensely he thought of ants marching under his skin.

Lettie slid her hands under the mattress and crawled the bed's perimeter. Zane focused on the dresser, scanning the surface and the corners of the drawers for any sneaky attempts at security. Sure enough, Guy had left two long pieces of dental floss hanging in front of the drawers. Zane lifted both and placed them carefully on the dresser top.

The first drawer contained balled-up socks, a four-pack of unopened energy drinks, body spray, condoms, some charger cords, and a pocketknife. Zane stared at the items without touching any of them, wondering why any of it warranted the protection of the dental floss trap. But it was likely that anyone snooping would start at the top drawers and work their way down, so maybe it was just a precaution. He opened the next drawer, which was filled with neat piles of men's bikini underwear in bright colors that reminded Zane of a candy store. He pressed down on the stacks, feeling for something hard like a box or weapon or something but nothing was there.

He shut the second drawer and reopened the first one. This time, he pulled the drawer all the way out and looked on the sides and back for something hidden. He came up short. Then he lifted the drawer up to look underneath. Ding ding ding! Jackpot for Zane. There was a brown paper envelope taped to the bottom of the drawer with duct tape. Using the small knife, he peeled a corner of the duct tape back and turned the envelope over to undo its metal clasp.

"What did you find?" Lettie said from over his shoulder.

Zane slid the envelope contents out into his hand. There was a U.S. passport in the name of Charvis Steen and penciled on the front page was a street address in Contra Costa, California. The unsmiling photo resembled Guy if he'd grown his hair into a mullet and gained a few pounds. Zane snapped a quick photo of the passport then put it back into the envelope, returned the envelope to the bottom of the drawer, and smoothed the duct tape securely against the wood. He eyed the returned envelope—it looked untouched to him. Hopefully, he hadn't used some kind of magical duct tape that revealed fingerprints in bright flashing colors after a few hours. He'd be up shit creek if that were the case. Or maybe Mrs. Ahern would be.

The bottom of the second drawer had another envelope,

this one containing two credit cards and a driver's license from Nevada with an address in Reno, the same date of birth as the passport, and a new name: Artemis Croxton. This guy certainly had a flair for dramatic names. Zane would have thought it would be better to pick aliases that didn't stick out like Charvis and Artemis but what did he know about the world of con men? Again, he took more photos of the credit cards and ID then replaced them carefully. Thirty minutes had passed. He checked the four remaining drawers but found nothing remarkable. When he finished, he retrieved the two pieces of dental floss and lay them across the drawer edges once again.

Fast footsteps came down the hall and Zane heard a hiss outside the door. Adrenaline flooded through him like water from a fire hose, and his heart went into overdrive.

"Zane, they're back!" Mrs. Ahern whispered, her voice hoarse and stricken. Zane scanned the room. Everything looked like it had when they came in. He put his fingers to his lips and eased open the door, gesturing for Lettie to follow him. To exit the mobile home through the back door, they needed to make the dash through the eat-in kitchen and through the laundry room but to do so, he and Lettie would be fully visible to anyone entering the living room. Footsteps sounded on the steps outside the front door and Zane decided it wasn't worth the risk. He pointed at the spare bedroom on the other side. Lettie slipped inside and he relocked Guy's door trying to keep his hands from shaking and jingling the key ring.

The spare room was overly warm, dark, and obviously used for storage from the most recent warehouse shopping run. Mrs. Ahern had enough paper towels and toilet paper to last a year stacked by the door. Zane flicked on the flashlight and scanned the room to see a cheap pressboard desk and plastic chair, the stackable kind they sell at the drug store or home goods store for a few dollars. Zane smelled laundry soap and camphor, maybe from mothballs. A long spiderweb strand hung down from the ceiling and tickled Zane's cheek.

There was a window, but Zane was afraid that the sound of opening it would call attention, and there still was the problem of the screen and the leap down. Not an option. He could hear voices growing louder as Guy and Emmaline moved into the living room. He and Lettie stood near the closed door, afraid to move lest they set off the squeaky foundation springs or make other noises that would give them away. He clicked the flashlight off and slipped it back in his pocket, hearing Lettie's breathing turn shallow and quick.

"Stay calm," he whispered, not sure if he was saying it to reassure her or himself. They would look pretty silly if Guy or Emmaline decided to open the spare room door for some reason and find Zane and Lettie standing there like idiots in the dark. What would he say? Tag, you're it? It was a ridiculous situation.

The voices in the living room drew closer and Zane heard Guy unlock his bedroom door. Emmaline giggled about something, then the bedroom door shut, and the lock clicked into place. More giggling from Emmaline. Zane wanted to clear his throat but resisted the urge. He listened intently for several minutes: no giggling, no chit-chat, no movement seemed to be coming from the opposite bedroom, and Zane wondered if he should have actually taken the passport and driver's license to make sure Guy didn't use them.

Then he heard the bed springs squeak and a low moan of pleasure he recognized as Emmaline's. *Oh, no.* He was not going to listen to Emmaline and Guy have sex. No way.

"Let's get out of here," he whispered. "Fast and quiet." He eased the door open and walked softly out of the room, Lettie on his heels. Mrs. Ahern was in the kitchen, peering out the back door. She looked at them with wide, terrified eyes and

Zane put his finger to his lips asking for her silence. Zane and Lettie made it all the way to the front door and were just about to push through the screen door when he heard Guy's bedroom door lock click again.

Mrs. Ahern came running out of the kitchen, her hands splayed on either side of her face like the kid in *Home Alone*. The door opened and Guy popped out of the bedroom and headed for the bathroom, bare-chested and barefoot. Dark hairs covered his slight potbelly, and his nipples were an odd shade of orange. Zane thanked his lucky stars that the man had pulled on sweatpants, so he didn't have to see the bikini underwear in three dimensions.

"Hello, Mrs. Ahern!" Lettie said, pivoting to make it look like she was arriving and not leaving. "I brought Zane over to look at that faucet leak you mentioned."

Zane offered a prayer up for his sister's quick-thinking mind and he thought he saw Mrs. Ahern do the same.

Guy turned in surprise. "I could have helped you with that." He smiled pleasantly at the three of them. "I'm very handy."

"Oh, I hate to bother you, Guy. You do so much already!" Mrs. Ahern said. "And I just mentioned it to Lettie. It's in here, in the master bath, Zane." She was better at improvising than Zane expected. Guy shrugged and flicked on the bathroom light and fan, glancing over his shoulder. Zane saw him pause and he followed Guy's gaze to the spare bedroom door. He and Lettie had forgotten to close it behind them when they exited. The door had been shut when Guy arrived and open when he came out just a few minutes later.

Zane's heart leapt into action so fast it was like falling down a flight of stairs. Guy stared at the door like it was a puzzle, his eyes narrowed, and arm still outstretched toward the bathroom light switch. Zane tried to act nonchalant and took a few small steps toward Mrs. Ahern. Then he saw Guy give a small shrug, shake his head, and walk into the bathroom.

"Good job," Zane told Mrs. Ahern as the three of them stood on a puffy pink throw rug in her tidy master bathroom, looking at the white pedestal sink and the faucet that clearly had no leak.

Mrs. Ahern stared at her reflection in the mirror and patted at her hair. "I don't like this."

The room smelled of rose air freshener and damp towels. Lettie ran her finger over a dusty pink candle sitting on the counter. "Isn't it even the tiniest bit exciting? Like being a spy?"

"No, not at all. How long should we wait?" Mrs. Ahern checked her thin gold watch, so small Zane didn't know how she could tell the time on it.

"Until he goes back in the room," Zane said. "Then we can leave out the back."

A few minutes later, that was exactly what they did. Lettie and Zane burst through the back door of Mrs. Ahern's house into the small yard, laughing. It was fun to flirt with danger and play spy, especially now that they got away with it.

"No wonder you like working in law enforcement," Lettie said. "That was thrilling."

"And you were right. There is something fishy about Guy Callahan, all right. Most people don't have passports and driver's licenses in more than one name."

"I'm not glad about that, for Emmaline, but I do feel vindicated. I thought there was something off with him, and I like knowing I'm right."

"I don't know what he's up to, but we're going to find out," Zane said.

Chapter 20
Zane

Zane drove to the library on Wednesday mid-morning to meet with Tyler Swinton. He returned Verda's book about Ecuador and a hefty novel with a swooning couple on the front. She loved books she called bodice-rippers with a bit of spice and was at the library every week or so exchanging one title for another.

One of the public computers in the reading room was occupied by a man in his late thirties, though from his weathered and suntanned face and layers of clothing that seemed too heavy for the balmy April weather outside, he may have been experiencing homelessness. Living rough like that tended to make people look ten years past their actual ages. Zane tried to make eye contact, but the man remained hunched, his shoulders blocking the screen for a bit of privacy.

Zane walked over to an empty table and pulled out a purple-cushioned chair. He'd arrived fifteen minutes earlier than the arranged meeting time between Swinton and Kayla so he could scope out the place and get a read on Swinton before he realized there was a switch. Getting him to the library had been easy enough—Zane pretended to be Kayla, ready to do her interview for the job, and Swinton bit right away, agreeing to meet in Tulsa. The library seemed like a safe, public setting.

Except for the man on the computer, the reading room was empty and darkening as spring storm clouds gathered outside the large picture windows. Zane felt agitated and invigorated, imagining Swinton's reaction when he learned he would be meeting with Zane and not Kayla. Would Swinton try to leave? Zane thought about what he would do in that situation. Would he chase after him out of the library and confront him in the parking lot? Would he block his path? Zane's leg muscles twitched with the thought.

The man at the computer looked up, as though sensing Zane's excitement. He studied Zane for a moment, his eyes edged with deep crow's feet, thin colorless lips pressed together, then returned his attention to the screen. He had several plastic bags at his feet, the brown plastic kind from the supermarket, and each were stuffed full with papers and clothes and tied at the top. Zane had a lot of empathy for the man and people like him, urban nomads on the fringes, wandering through public spaces with no particular place to call home other than maybe a car. If it weren't for his grandmother, he and Lettie might have found themselves in a similar situation a few times.

Swinton walked in a few moments later. Zane watched him trace the perimeter of the library, soft footsteps on carpet drowned out by the whir of the copy machine. He looked at Swinton's bulbous eyes, fleshy cheeks, scant hair, and saggy shoulders down to his scuffed white Adidas. He looked too weak-livered to be a cold-blooded killer, but the police academy and Loris had warned him time and again to never make assumptions like that. Desperate people do desperate things and underestimating a person's capacity for violence when cornered was not a good idea.

Having made a complete round of the library, Swinton stopped at the opening of the reading room and took out his phone. Zane stood up and strode over to him.

"You're here to meet Kayla, right? She sent me." Zane gestured to the table like he was inviting Swinton into his home. "Come sit and talk with me."

Swinton stood with his fingers wrapped around his phone, scowling at Zane. Like Sherwood Rittenhour, Swinton had adopted that tech CEO uniform of long-sleeved black T-shirt and jeans, with the addition of a small diamond stud earring in his right ear. A piece of thin red string was tied around his left wrist.

"Let's talk," Zane repeated, aware that the man at the computer was watching their interaction with interest.

Swinton blew out enough breath to inflate a balloon and sat down at the table, the chair squeaking as he dropped into the seat. He laid his phone face down on the table. "This better be good," he said. "And who are you?" His eyes had the brightness of a day drinker just starting on a binge and his words blurred together softly.

"Zane Clearwater. I'm working for a private detective called Loris Trapper. Kayla hired us to help her with a private matter." He paused to see if his name or Loris' earned any type of reaction from Swinton but saw nothing other than irritation.

"What's the private matter?"

"That's the thing about private matters," Zane said. "They're private. But she and I have some questions we'd like you to answer." He slid a stick of gum across the table at the man. "Maybe you want to freshen your breath a bit. Smells like you got an early start at the bar."

Swinton's nostrils flared like an angry bull about to charge.

His jaw flexed like he was going to say something, and Zane felt squirmy inside but tried to stay cool. Had he not played it cool enough?

Then Tyler seemed to change his mind. He unwrapped the gum and popped it into his mouth. "This is a highly unusual job interview. Look, I thought this young woman had a nice way about her and that I might be able to help her get out of that minimum wage job at the Boot Barn. Now I'm catfished into meeting with a private detective and I think I ought to leave."

Nice try, Zane thought. Swinton almost summoned up enough outrage to be believable in his protest, but something lurked behind those watery eyes that told Zane to press on.

"I've got a bunch of questions for you. First, why did you try several times to see Dawn Renee at the Pickert Real Estate office in Tulsa? Next up, tell me how you knew Diana Granger in the spring of 2001. I'm also curious if you knew who Kayla Renee was before you met her at the Boot Barn. And finally, I'm really wondering if you saw our ads looking for information about Diana or Dawn. And if you did, how come you didn't respond?"

"I've got a question for you. Are you the one who convinced the police I had something to do with this woman's murder? They've been hounding me for days and I've got to tell you, you're not a very good interrogator. You haven't even asked me about my whereabouts the night she died. That seems like question number one. And the answer is: with my in-laws." Swinton reached for his phone but instead of opening an app or texting, he just stared at the dark screen like he was trying to decide what to do. It was a good sign. Swinton was stalling for time.

"Let's start with my last question. Did you see our ads all over social looking for information about Diana Granger? We know for a fact you worked closely with her. We have a witness who knew you both back then at WorthComm." Zane pushed a print copy of Dawn Renee's photograph toward Swinton.

He picked the photo up and gave it a close look. "Sure, I recognize her. I'm not denying I used to know Diana Granger."

He dropped the photo just as Loris approached the table holding a tissue in an outstretched hand. "There is no gum chewing in the library," she said in her best librarian voice. "Please spit it out in this tissue and give it to me."

Zane held his breath, trying to mirror the surprised and amused smile crossing Swinton's face. "I feel like I'm in kindergarten," he said, but he took the grey gum wad out of his mouth with pinched fingers and wrapped the tissue around it. His hand shook as he dropped the gum into Loris's open palm.

"Thank you," she said, pivoting on her heel toward the front of the library.

"You betcha," Swinton said. "I used to have a girlfriend who worked in a library. Sexy as hell."

Gross, Zane thought. He didn't want to hear about this loser's love life or wild librarian fantasies. "So, when did you meet Diana Granger?"

"I don't know when exactly. Sometime around the Christmas holiday in 2001. Not long after 9/11, I remember. My God, that was twenty-three years ago."

"Where did you meet her?"

"At WorthComm. We were both fairly new employees in the business development department back then."

"Did she work for you?"

"Yes, as part of a team. Me and her and another guy. We had to go around to chamber and business mixer events, meet people, try to present WorthComm like it was some good citizen while looking for business opportunities. Lots of cocktail parties and long lunches."

"Were you romantically involved with her?"

Swinton took a swallow. "No. I had my hands full. I was in my mid-thirties. I had been at Enron and lost everything—my entire pension plan, all my stock was worthless—when I landed at WorthComm. I was having a mid-life crisis I guess—bored of the wife-and-baby routine at home, so I got tangled up with another woman. Not Diana. She was like my little protege, fresh out of college, full of promise and I just liked her. Looked out for her. That's all."

"When did you last see her?"

"She just disappeared one day. Said something about needing to be with family, quit the job without even two weeks' notice if I remember right."

"Was she pregnant?"

Swinton tapped the pen on the table, and from another room, Zane could hear the swish of a backpack zipper opening. He looked at Zane, opened his mouth and shut it, tapped his fingers against the table, and looked at Zane again.

"Yes, she was eating for two. So she said."

"And you were the baby daddy."

"Not me. She wouldn't tell me who the father was, and she said she planned on getting an abortion."

"She did not get an abortion. Does that surprise you?"

"So that's what this is about."

"Would you be interested in a DNA test to determine if you are in fact the father of this child? She is now twenty-two years old."

"And her name is Kayla. Got it. You're thinking it's too much of a coincidence that I just happened to run into her at the Boot Barn and offer her a job."

"It does strike me as particularly unlikely, for a lot of reasons."

"What if I was just looking out for the daughter of an old friend? Wanting to help doesn't make me her father."

"So, you knew Diana Granger had changed her name to Dawn Renee?"

"I did but only recently. I ran into her by chance at some Fort Worth steakhouse one night. I was there with Sherwood Rittenhour. Do you know him? He's the CEO of WorthComm. He's worth about a billion dollars. Maybe more. And his venture capital firm is a silent investor in my company. He invited me out to dinner, and it turned out to be some "come to Jesus" meeting where he was trying to blame me for market conditions. It's tough out there. This country's practically in a recession. Every business is hurting. Then out of the blue, there's Diana. Neither of us had seen her in years. I was relieved to see her because I didn't want to hear any more of his bullshit. People like him just love to hear themselves talk. But she hightailed out of there like an antelope with a cheetah on its heels. Made a spectacle of herself and left her friend all alone. That friend of Diana's is the woman who told us her name was Dawn and that she had a daughter, and so I did some digging."

"That made you think you were on the hook for child support?"

"No. I'm not the father. But I cared about Diana, so I called her a few weeks later at her office and talked to her. I asked her if she needed help and she said no. So, I let it go. Kayla could have asked me this herself. I was going to..."

He swallowed his next words instead of saying them. Then he changed the subject. "You said you wanted to know why I came to see Dawn. I wanted to hire her, that's all. I'm trying to get this company off the ground, and we could use someone like her. She wasn't interested."

"Why would that make you so angry that the receptionist said he picked up the phone to call security?"

"I wasn't angry. I was annoyed. Dawn thought she was some big shot, couldn't even come to the lobby to talk to me for old time's sake? Nothing I hate more than people flexing how busy they are, like some dystopian status symbol."

"Maybe she was under a lot of pressure," Zane said. "Have the police asked you where you were the night of her boyfriend's death? Did you know Gabriel Connor?"

Swinton made a low, theatrical groan and his voice became belligerent. "Maybe I'm too busy for this conversation. You're a sleazy liar and probably an extortionist too. I'm done talking." He rose from the chair, pressing his hands into the reading table for leverage. When he stood, he uttered some more insults in a voice loud enough to make the man at the computer glare at them.

He strode out of the library with heavy footsteps. Zane pulled out his phone and texted Loris that Swinton had left the building. His distaste for Swinton's character ran deep and he was sure the man had been lying to him about wanting to "look out" for Diana. Zane suspected that he had been Diana's lover, not friend. This suspicion made him feel sorry for Kayla. If she had known what she was going to get for her money, maybe she wouldn't have hired them. But there was the matter of the cryptocurrency. A million dollars or close to it would sweeten the revelation that her likely father, Tyler Swinton, was an asshole of tremendous magnitude.

As he passed the banks of computers on his way out of the library, the man who had been watching them swiveled his neck to eye Zane. "If you want to know what I think, I'll tell you."

Zane paused in his stride. "I'm listening."

"He's lying to you. That yelling at the end, pure showmanship."

Zane grinned. "Kind of what I thought too." He fist-bumped the man and went out to his car to call Loris.

"I'm just pulling into the DNA lab parking lot now," she said. "Did you like my librarian act?"

"Not important what I thought, but Swinton fell for it. I couldn't believe he spat the gum out and gave it to you. I was pretty sure it wasn't going to work."

"I was channeling my old second-grade teacher," she said. "Being a woman of a certain age has its moments."

"How long will it take to get the lab to test the gum for DNA and compare the results to Curtis Rittenhour?"

"I'm going to ask them to do it as fast as they can. Any theories?"

"I'd lay money down that he's Kayla's father and he knows about that Bitcoin. He said he wanted to hire her but maybe he really wanted funding for his company, and she shined him on."

"Makes sense to me. We'll see what the DNA says," Loris said. "Hey, do me a favor, will you? Can you run by the Antoinette Bakery?"

"Sure, is that the one in the Arts District?"

"That's the one. Drop by and have them send a Snickers tart to Jennette Felton as a thank you. If she won't take reward money, she'll certainly take some butter and sugar and that tart is as close to heaven as I'm going to get."

Chapter 21
Lettie

Artemis Croxton and Charvis Steen had to be the stupidest fake names Lettie had ever heard. She typed the names into Duck Duck Go—the search engine that didn't track your every digital move like Google— but the results were poor. Searching "Charvis Steen" pulled up information on some rich dude named Charles Steen who owned uranium mines and a $30 million horse ranch in Utah. "Artemis Croxton" brought up cryptocurrency information as well as articles about NASA's Artemis mission to the moon in 2022. The cryptocurrency stuff popped out like a bright flag, but it turned out to be nothing more than another platform for trading the stuff. She resisted the temptation to read about the Artemis mission and switched to Google.

Google brought up different and more varied types of wrong answers: an inactive Instagram profile called artemis_crock featuring videos of members of the Stray Kids KPOP band, an interview with an author named Artemis Crow, and a GameSpot page on the comic book character

Artemis Crock. Rabbit holes. She scrolled and scrolled and scrolled. Now that Google had done away with organizing results in pages, the search results generated a seemingly infinite list of web links. None seemed helpful.

Of course, there were the usual ads for websites advertising services to find people. Most were pay-to-play, Lettie knew, and not worth the money. They typically searched the free state and federal agency databases a smart web user could find with a little digging at usa.gov. Maybe she should check out the California databases to see if she could search that state's criminal records or incarceration like she could in Oklahoma.

It was a dead-end. California, unlike Oklahoma, said criminal history records were not "subject to disclosure" under the Public Records Act. The state's website went on to say that "In California, state and local summary criminal history information is confidential and access is strictly regulated by statute."

Fine. Maybe it was something she could ask Zane to do using the networks he and Loris could tap into as private investigators. Still, most people these days left some kind of digital trace of their movements and their lives. Guy Callahan or Artemis Croxton or Charvis Steen had to have left footprints somewhere on the interwebs, and if he had, Lettie was going to find them.

She grabbed her phone and scrolled through comments left on Emmaline's Instagram posts to see if Guy was following her there and liking her posts like any good boyfriend would do. Sure enough, she found a comment on Emmaline's most recent post about the benefits of drinking kombucha by @theguyyouknow reading "smoking hot" with at least a dozen flame emojis. She clicked through to @theguyyouknow's profile. The profile had a photo, but it wasn't of Guy's face. Instead, he had chosen a photo of that brown Shiba Inu that had been a huge meme known as "Doge" several years ago. The meme played off the dog's silly expression and the misspelling of the word "dog." Just Internet silliness really. The account didn't have the hallmarks of a fake account, though. He had more than two hundred followers and about the same number of people he was following. About twenty-five posts populated the profile grid, but none were very recent. The first post had been made in 2019 so it wasn't a brand-new account.

She took a closer look at the first post. The date on it was May 25, 2018. The post was the only one on the grid that featured people—it appeared to be a family photo. A younger version of Guy sat in a diner booth next to an older couple who seemed the right age to be his grandparents. The caption read "The pancakes at Sugar Plum Coffee Shop always hit the spot," and Guy had obligingly allowed Instagram to tag the restaurant's Concord, California location. Mrs. Ahern had said Guy was from Concord.

Excited, Lettie scrolled through usernames of the people who had liked the post, her finger hovering over an account with the username @CatherineJim that had commented with a series of red heart emojis. The profile for @CatherineJim mainly featured photos of flowers taken in a garden: lilies, lilacs, roses. All had the Concord geo-tag. And Guy Callahan was following @CatherineJim.

Lettie felt a little tingle. She was getting somewhere. She was sure of it. On a whim, she typed "Catherine Callahan of Concord, California," into Google. It was a lot of what her English teacher would call alliteration, Lettie thought, proud to have remembered the term for when a sentence contains a series of words starting with the same letter.

"Bingo!" she said when Google returned an obituary for someone named Mary Callahan who died at age 45 in 2019 and was survived by her parents Catherine and Jim Callahan of Concord, a son named Gordon, and a daughter named Augustina. Her next search gave her a phone number for a James G. Callahan on Elm Drive in Concord. She picked up her phone, dialed *67 so her number would come up as private on the other end, then punched in the numbers. As she heard it ring, she wondered what she would say if someone picked up.

"Hello?" It was a woman's voice, elderly.

"Hello," Lettie said. "I'm trying to reach Guy Callahan."

There was a silence. "Can you hold on for a moment?" The woman must have put the phone down on a table or something, and in the background, Lettie could hear muffled conversation followed by silence.

Then a man picked up the phone, asking, "May I help you?"

"Guy?" Lettie said.

"Who is calling?" the man asked. His tone was cautious, as though she were a scammer trying to steal their identities.

"Um, yeah, this is Ali Pointer," Lettie said, her mind supplying the name of a girl in one of her online classes as an alias. "This isn't Guy, is it? Do I have the wrong number?"

"How did you get this number?"

"I found it on the internet." It wasn't a lie. "Guy told me he had grandparents living in Concord, so I just did some searching and found this. See, the mobile number he gave me isn't working and he's not answering my messages on social media, so I thought I'd call here. I met him recently and I need to talk to him."

"He's not here," the man said. "What do you need to talk to him for?"

"Oh, is he still in Oklahoma, do you know? I thought maybe he might have gone back to California."

"Just a minute." The man must have placed his palm over

the landline mouthpiece and Lettie could hear indistinct voices having another conversation.

The man returned to the phone. "Why don't you give me your name and number and I'll have him get back to you?"

"Sure, that's fine," Lettie said. She gave the fake name again, taking a lot of time to explain how Ali was spelled with one "i" and not two and then making up a phone number. "Do you think I should mail this stuff he left or just hang on to it? I'd feel badly if he thought he lost it."

"What stuff?"

"Um, clothes, mainly. A pair of jeans and a few T-shirts, but I know he really likes the blue one because he was wearing it all the time. And there was a hundred-dollar bill in his jeans. I don't want him to think I stole it or anything like that. Do you expect to see him anytime soon?"

A short pause, then a curt tone. "Who is this exactly?"

Lettie hung up in a panic. So much for trying to wing it as an investigator and trying to fool old Grandma and Grandpa. She couldn't imagine what Guy was up to, but she sure didn't like the sound of Emmaline taking this random guy on as any sort of manager. Emmaline was so taken with this man—Guy could probably talk her into anything. Why did she have such bad taste in men? Guy was moving quickly too, and Lettie thought she and Zane better come up with some answers before things got too far along.

She turned her attention back to the obituary again, re-reading the names listed as survivors. When her mobile phone rang moments later, she jumped. Had she misdialed the *67 and exposed her phone number? Were the Callahan's calling back?

One glance at the phone put her mind at ease as Angel's photo appeared as caller ID.

"Hi baby," she said.

"Hey, how's it going?" His voice was distant and soft. She filled him in on the latest about Guy Callahan and he made all the right noises and comments like he was listening, but she knew him well. He had something on his mind, and she might as well let him get to it.

"So, what's up?" she asked.

"I want to talk seriously about this move," he said. "And I want you to listen to me."

"Oh, Angel, we've talked and talked about it. I'm tired of hearing about it."

"No, you've talked about it, and I've talked about it, but we talk past each other. I understand how you feel. I know you're scared. But I've thought about this long and hard, and I want to do it. This is our path to financial security, Lettie. And it's my decision to make. I'm going to tell Atomic Video Games yes. They've agreed to pay for a hotel room for you whenever you want to come and stay. And the money is good and it's going to lead to more. So, I'm saying yes."

Lettie's anger rose like a wave, and she snorted with derision. "Oh really? And I'm just supposed to say okay, whatever you want, Angel, honey, that's fine?"

"You should say how you feel, and I should say how I feel. I think you've been dismissive of this idea and refusing to see its potential. I love you and I love Milly, and I don't understand how you cannot see that this is the best thing for us. Long-term."

"Okay, I guess there's nothing more for me to say." The words tasted bitter to her. "Don't expect me to show up in Oklahoma City just because you decided to do this."

"You're angry," he said. "I shouldn't have tried to do this on the phone. It's just that the team is pressuring me a bit over here. Let's let things cool off and talk some more later when I'm home."

"Easy for you to say. You're getting what you want."

She hung up the phone and flung it on the floor. She was all fury and nerves, feeling like they were accelerating toward something bad, and she wasn't quite sure how soon they would get there.

Chapter 22
Zane

Old Spice called with the news that Tyler Swinton had been brought in for questioning as a "person of interest" around the same time the laboratory called Loris with the results from the gum DNA test. It seemed that a neighbor's security videos rescued from deletion on the cloud showed Swinton visiting Dawn's home three times in the weeks leading up to her death, including the night she died. The police hadn't tied him to the succinylcholine yet, but they felt it was only a matter of time.

The police closing in on Swinton didn't surprise him, but the DNA test results did. Swinton was related to Kayla but not as a father. As an uncle. His DNA lined up with Dawn's as having the same mother and father—and here was the big shocker—they were both part of the Rittenhour family tree. Dawn/Diana and Swinton were brother and sister, and Curtis looked to be their half-brother. Why hadn't Swinton told him this? Why would he want to kill his sister?

Zane's brain was ping-ponging around with the latest revelations, trying to figure out how it all made sense. He knew enough to do one thing. When he heard on the news that Tyler Swinton might soon be arrested, he drove out to Uncle Brian and Aunt Tracy's home to tell Kayla Renee. Of course, when they offered him fresh fried catfish and corn pudding, he couldn't say no.

After lunch, he told Kayla the news about Swinton. The shock of knowing she had let her mom's killer get close enough to touch her rendered her speechless for a few beats and after that it was a floodgate of questions. Naturally, she wanted to know what had happened and why he wanted to kill her mom. Zane knew he had been stalling Kayla for a few days and she had a right to know, but the truth was he didn't know anything more concrete than those two facts.

"He's my uncle? Why would he kill my mom? Do you think he wanted the crypto wallet?" Kayla was blinking so fast he thought she might be on the verge of fainting like a Victorian lady in the movies. "That's got to be it. Do you think he has the password?"

"I don't know," Zane said for what felt like the twelfth time. She wanted to go back home but he insisted she stay a few more nights in Wagoner, just in case. By the time he left, he was pretty sure she no longer thought he was the perfect person to solve this mystery for her, but she didn't have many other options at this point.

Back at the office, he read every word he could find about the latest in the investigation. Someone had leaked that the police were looking hard at Tyler Swinton. People on Twitter and the true crime and Tulsa news sub-reddits were speculating about Swinton and Dawn Renee being lovers and that her death was a crime of passion, but Zane knew the truth of their relationship. There was some new information about Tyler Swinton and one item that teased at a motive related to needing money. Six months ago, Swinton had tried to raise another round of funds for his start-up without any luck. It seemed he had burned through the first round of cash but couldn't get the second round to come through. He was keeping the company going, but things weren't looking good for Valor Medicine for Men.

Other things Zane learned didn't clear up the central mystery of why Swinton killed Dawn, but they did tell him more about the man. For example, that he had never achieved distinction in business or anywhere, never quite getting the timing right or bringing anything successfully across the finish line. It didn't seem like anyone who met him had ever been impressed. His ex-wives, who must have been impressed enough once to marry him, had lost that feeling long ago. The other thing Zane learned was that the Rittenhour connection was a secret. There was no public evidence or even rumors that Sherwood Rittenhour had two children with a woman other than his wife.

When the second call came from Old Spice on Saturday, Zane was packing up his desk to get home for bingo night babysitting, and Loris was doing expense reports.

"Zane Clearwater here," he said in his most chipper voice.

"Is Loris there with you?" the detective said.

"She is." Zane flicked the desk phone onto speaker. "It's Detective Pastor calling."

Loris rolled her chair across the floor until her armrest bumped up against his and raised her eyebrows. "Yes, Angus?"

"About Tyler Swinton."

"Sure."

"We think he's the guy but most of our evidence is circumstantial. I've got some info to share with you but it's confidential."

"We're listening, but why are you willing to tell us?" If

Loris was fishing for a compliment from Old Spice, she wasn't going to get it, Zane knew.

"Do you want the info or not?"

"Yes," Loris and Zane said at the same time.

"He had money problems. You probably figured that out already. They go back years and years. Three mortgages on the house, financial backers melting away. We found evidence in his house that he had gone heavily into cryptocurrency a while back. Turned out to be his one good investment, but this guy spends money like it is water, so he'd run through most of it. Apparently, he'd given some of it to Dawn Renee about ten years ago. We found emails to her going back at least a year asking for that money back. She would reply with either a one-word answer or when she got fed up, two words. Guess which two those were."

"Up yours?" Zane quipped.

Old Spice snorted. "Yeah, sorta like that but even more direct. Not a lot of brother-sister love between these two. Anyway, the cryptocurrency. As far as why he gave it to Dawn Renee, he never says in the emails and neither does she. So, we've got a motive for Tyler Swinton to want to kill her. It's a little fuzzy as to why he gave her that money in the first place."

"That's something anyway, though not as much I would have hoped for. But I thank you for the information," Loris said. "We appreciate it. What about Gabriel Connor? Did Swinton kill him too?"

"We're looking into it. Swinton was in Fort Worth the night Connor died, so it doesn't seem likely. On that note, I've got to go. Remember how I helped you out," Old Spice said and hung up.

"It's a long shot but maybe Swinton has the PIN," Zane said. "We could go and talk to him."

"He's not going to be willing to do that yet," Loris said. "But I've got a different idea. Let's get Rittenhour on the phone."

"Father or son?"

"Sherwood. The father."

Zane flipped through his notebook to find the number they'd used to get Rittenhour in his WorthComm office. On speakerphone, Loris navigated the automated answering system, the human call center operator, the executive office receptionist and finally Rittenhour's personal assistant.

"Tell him it's Loris Trapper again and we have most of the puzzle pieces in place now," she said.

"You'd do better to tell me a little bit more." Rittenhour's assistant sounded snooty and patronizing, as though she was talking to a small child who had smeared mud on the floor.

"Tell him we want to talk about Tyler Swinton," Zane said.

The assistant paused, and in the empty space, Zane wondered if news of the murder and Tyler Swinton's arrest had made the rounds of the executive office staff. He knew it was all over the WorthComm messaging boards online.

"Please hold," the assistant said. If Zane had been a betting man, he would have laid down a hundred dollars that the assistant knew exactly who Tyler Swinton was, based on how fast she gave in. He also would have bet more money that the next voice they heard would be her again, telling them goodbye and get lost. After all, this call was what someone might call a Hail Mary in football, where you just fling the ball toward the goal and hope for the best.

Zane would have lost the bet. He didn't time it because his mind was skipping all over the place, but it might have been two hours or two minutes when Rittenhour's voice growled at them through the phone's speaker.

"You are a piece of work," was all he said.

"Mr. Rittenhour?"

"It's not Santa Claus."

Loris snorted roughly. "I'll get right to it, then. I just spoke with the Tulsa Police about the investigation of the murder of Dawn Renee, who you know as Diana Granger. To justify a charge of first-degree murder the police aim to establish a motive. I think they would be very interested in your name so they can ask you about your relationship with Tyler Swinton and Diana. They may even need you to testify at his trial."

Only the sound of breathing came from Rittenhour's end of the phone.

Loris continued. "I have very good reasons to believe you might care to see that Tyler Swinton has the best possible defense."

"Has he asked for me?"

"No."

"I've told you what I know."

Loris's eyes narrowed as they roamed the room as though trying to see the truth. "Are you sure?"

"If I had known the day I got the call about that stupid piece of art..." Rittenhour didn't finish that sentence. "Fine, come by the house tomorrow morning."

"We don't have access to a private plane as you do, Mr. Rittenhour, and it is a five-hour drive. Perhaps you could find your way back to Tulsa tomorrow around ten? I can give you our address again."

"Dammit, I have your address from the first time you tricked me. Fine." He hung up.

Loris flung the phone on her desk and sank back in her chair.

"That was a gamble," Zane said. "I was sweating bullets."

"Me too but it was that or nothing."

"So, the plan is to get him to admit he is Dawn and Tyler's father then?"

"Yes. And to have Kayla here to listen to it. That will give her some answers."

"There's the matter of the cryptocurrency still." Zane frowned. "Rittenhour's not going to be able to help with the password, is he? And how is she going to pay?"

"Problems, problems, problems. One at a time, Zane. Isn't that what they say in AA? First, let's deliver Kayla's family tree to her. She has a right to know."

"It's one *day* at a time," Zane said. "Kayla is a nice person, and she's been a good client. Everything we've learned about this family just makes me sorrier."

"Yeah, it's a tough one," Loris said. "But she wanted to know. That's why she hired you."

Zane thought back, remembering his warnings to her about how sometimes secrets were kept quiet for a reason. His personal experience with his mother's private affairs made him sure that Kayla would rather know than not, but it didn't make it any easier to find a way to tell her. Loris was right. Why not let her hear it directly from Sherwood Rittenhour? They hadn't found her father or the PIN to the hard wallet, but they had found Kayla a grandfather and an uncle, awful as they were.

When Kayla arrived at the offices of Loris Trapper Investigations that morning, she made it clear she didn't expect to spend the following hour tucked into the server closet next to a tangle of wires and tall blinking computer towers. She whined and complained, especially when Loris took her mobile phone away and locked it in the safe so that she couldn't record what she was about to hear. But once she saw how firm they were that this was the only way to answer some of her questions, Kayla perched herself on the folding step stool that was the best seat Zane could find for her. She sat hunched over with her arms wrapped around her knees, looking expectant and emotional. Zane hoped she wouldn't decide to burst into the room and confront Sherwood directly as he wasn't sure what the man's reaction would be.

The first thing Zane noticed when Rittenhour walked into the office was how deflated he seemed. Everything about him seemed to sag: his black T-shirt was as wrinkled as his forehead, and he seemed smaller and older than before. They all said the "good mornings" as though this were any other meeting of friends, then Loris launched in.

"Thank you for coming on a Sunday and I'm sorry for the bullying to get you here. You're a smart man and a rich and powerful one, and yet you've decided to come here and talk."

"What do you want?"

"We want nothing but answers. We are only concerned with doing the work that our client, Kayla Renee, the daughter of Dawn Renee, hired us to do. We were hired to help her gain access to some money her mother left behind and secondarily, to help her understand her family tree. Your son Curtis obliged us with a DNA test that shows Kayla's definitely related to you and Curtis and Tyler. We thought at first that one of you was her father, but now we know that was wrong. In fact, you are Dawn Renee's father and Kayla's grandfather. And Tyler Swinton is also your son."

Rittenhour pinched his lips together and raised his chin as though ready for a punch. Zane swore he could see blood pumping through the vein in his neck.

"True," he said.

Loris nodded. "Did they know you were their father?"

"Yes, but not until they were adults. Their mother's name was Angela Swinton. She was a cocktail waitress in a bar in Fort Worth. She kept my identity a secret because I paid her well. She was a practical woman and I loved her, in my way.

When she died back in 2000, Tyler came to me, demanded I give them both money. I gave them jobs instead with enough salary that they'd continue to keep our relationship quiet. Do you have any more questions?"

"Why wasn't Diana a Swinton? What about Kayla's dad?"

"Diana tied the knot at seventeen, one of those impulsive young marriages. It crashed in nine months, but she held onto the Granger name and credit card bills."

"Who's Kayla's father?"

"No idea. Diana vanished in 2001. After that, no contact until the surprise meeting at that Fort Worth steakhouse. She never really forgave me for keeping her and Tyler hidden. It wasn't just about money to her, but the principle. 'Living a double life,' she'd chide me. Funny, given what she ended up doing."

"Our life's patterns get imprinted early on," Zane said.

Rittenhour pinned Zane with an ice-cold glare. "You like psychology? Here's my take. Tyler doesn't have the killer instinct in him. He didn't poison Diana. He loved her and looked out for her. He wasn't good at business, and he may have wanted money from her, but he wouldn't murder her to get it. If you two wanted to be helpful, you could get to work on finding the real culprit."

Loris cleared her throat. "And if you had wanted to be helpful, you could have saved the Tulsa Police, Kayla Renee, and us a lot of time and effort had you just been honest about your relationship to Dawn and Tyler from the start. If you'd like to pay us for that work so Kayla doesn't have to, we can return her retainer and charge her nothing. Should you decide to do that, the amount is ten thousand dollars plus whatever time it takes for us to try to clear Tyler's name."

"Do what you need to do. I'll pay."

Rittenhour left without another word before Loris could

try to wrangle his signature on a contract. "He'll pay," Loris said, waving off Zane's concerns.

Kayla emerged. Her cheeks had less color than usual. "So, you think my mother's killer is still out there?"

"Possibly," Loris said. "You heard everything?"

"Yes. I did. I think I want to go home."

"I'd rather you went back out to my uncle and aunt's. Just for the time being."

"Okay, but... I don't want to talk about this with you now. These people, they're awful... I'll call you later. I'll go back to Wagoner, but I'll drive myself. I need to clear my head."

Chapter 23
Zane

Zane cautiously observed the tranquil atmosphere in front of Gabriel Connor's south midtown apartment. His car was his covert command post as he silently studied the Colonial Apartments from afar. He worried Old Spice or another Tulsa PD officer was going to arrive and catch him at the scene which would not be good. For twenty minutes, he sat and observed the foot traffic patterns and saw no one other than a food delivery driver dropping off two enormous brown bags at the apartment next to Gabriel's. He took stock of his private investigator's kit: lock picks, a penlight, his phone for audio and video recording, and a pair of rubber gloves. The time for action was now.

He hoofed it to Gabriel's apartment like he was running late, noticing the dead plant on the windowsill of one of the occupants. A warning hung ominously from Gabriel's door, sealed off with a striking yellow cross of cautionary crime-scene tape. Disruption would not be tolerated by the Tulsa Police, it said. With a slight shrug of his shoulders, Zane carefully surveyed the area for any signs of life. Satisfied that he was alone and undetected, he put on rubber gloves before deftly using a pick to open the door in barely sixty seconds. Loris had made him practice on the office door until he had mastered the technique. He stepped through the door then turned and reattached the yellow tape at its seam, then shut the door quietly, his fingers trembling with anticipation. He would give himself twenty minutes for the search, thinking that even if a neighbor had seen him breaking in, it would take the Tulsa Police at least that long to respond.

The interior was dim. Gabriel's blinds were closed, and sunlight was blocked by the second-story overhang. A boxy living area/dining room gave way to a small and efficient kitchen, newly redone with white cabinets so bright they nearly gleamed in the dark. The furniture was utilitarian, masculine, and not cheap: black leather sofa, chrome, and glass coffee table, an 85-inch flat-screen television mounted on the wall. Triple monitors curved around a smooth white desk with black edging facing a black-and-red captain's chair that wouldn't have looked out of place on the Starship Enterprise. No doubt about it, this guy was a member of Lettie and Angel's gamer culture, and an affluent one at that.

Zane walked to a bronze telescope set on a tripod in the left corner of the dining area and peered through the lens. All he saw was the flat white of the closed mini-blinds. He didn't dare open them to see what Gabriel had the telescope trained on as he didn't want to give away his presence. The dining room table was glass and chrome and four bentwood chairs sat around it like obedient small children. A stack of old mail sat in the center, and Zane flipped through it quickly hoping to find a cellphone bill or bank statement but no luck. After all, the police had already been through the apartment, and they wouldn't have missed anything like that.

Zane would have to get wildly lucky to find something useful.

A granite counter spanned one wall of the kitchen, surrounded on top and bottom by beveled white cabinets with graceful, smooth silver handles. Only a dirty coffee mug and spoon sat in the sink from Gabriel's last breakfast on earth. Stove, refrigerator, microwave, coffee maker, a glass cookie jar with an opened bag of Milanos cookies inside, all relatively new. No kitchen window. On the counter, a box of frosted cereal flakes, open but with the top carefully closed with those small cardboard tabs, and a large bottle of multivitamins. The upper cabinets contained plain white dishes, bowls, and coffee mugs and an assortment of reusable water bottles in a rainbow of colors, each advertising a different video game or technology company. A tall pantry-style cabinet had bottles of wine, more Frosted Flakes cereal, a box of cheese crackers, green tea bags, some powdered creamer, and ten cans of Dinty Moore stew. Someone must be a fan. Under the kitchen sink, Zane found the discarded ends of three smoked marijuana joints and an empty can of Dinty Moore. A bottle of window cleaner and another of drain cleaner were all he had by way of cleaning supplies, making Zane think he must have hired someone to clean the place. The refrigerator had expensive bottled Fiji water, a dozen yogurts, some apples, lunchmeat, a loaf of wheat bread, and a jar of natural peanut butter, separated such that an inch of oil lay on top of the peanut butter sludge. Zane resisted the temptation to pull the peanut butter out of the fridge. Gabriel wouldn't be worrying about tearing the bread with cold peanut butter spread now.

Between the living area and back wall of the kitchen was the door to the bedroom, with a closet and small bathroom tucked inside. A black ceiling fan with sharp-looking blades hung over a king-sized bed covered in a grey comforter. An old-fashioned metal lamp sat on the nightstand on the right side, alongside a bright blue case holding one of those rubber mouth guards meant to keep people from grinding their teeth at night, and a science fiction book with a sexy blue female alien on the cover. The dresser had the usual T-shirts, socks, and boxers, and the bedside table included condoms, foot cream, and a pink silk eye mask and matching hair scrunchie. Had those been Dawn's? Other than those two items, there was little to suggest of a regular female visitor spending the night in this man cave.

Time was ticking. Zane felt a flurry of anxiety as he saw ten minutes had passed since he entered. He caught a glimpse of his face in Gabriel's mirror: he looked pasty and worried. In the distance, a trailer-truck blew its horn. Zane felt his breath quicken. What was he missing? He had to think like someone with something to hide. The police had undoubtedly covered this ground multiple times before sealing the apartment.

He looked in the closet. A dry cleaner's bag held a dark blue suit. Also hanging in the closet were a couple pairs of jeans, a few long-sleeve shirts, a bright red OU sweatshirt, and a dark orange fleece jacket. So, Gabriel was a Sooner. Zane was not learning anything useful and began to regret taking this risk.

The most obvious hiding places such as under the bed, back of the couch, in a fake can of soup, in the freezer, had undoubtedly been exhausted by the police. Zane would have to think differently. He went into the bathroom and examined the pipes leading from the toilet tank to the wall. Why were there two? He grabbed the longer piece of white PVC, about two inches in diameter and peered into it. Nothing. But clearly a hiding place, as the pipe had no other purpose. This gave him hope. He tried not to think about the grossness of his face hovering this man's bathroom floor as he pressed his ear against the baseboard of the bathroom, searching for clues of hidden stashes concealed behind false walls. His tapping revealed nothing but solid wood. He opened the cabinet under the sink, removed the spare toilet paper rolls, looking in each to see if anything was hidden in the cardboard tubes. Nothing again.

Zane shined his penlight from corner to corner, uncovering a mysterious dark wood rear wall with four screw heads, each set in its own corner. Convinced that something was hidden behind the partition, he grabbed hold of his trusty screwdriver and started twisting away at the screws until it gave way beneath gentle pressure. To his gratification, there lay a cavity six inches deep. Along the bottom lay a folded white shirt or jacket, made from the kind of cloth used in uniforms. Zane gingerly lifted the item from the space and unfolded it. It was a jacket, not a shirt, the kind doctors or pharmacists might wear. It had the logo of St. Francis Hospital on it and clipped to it was a name badge in a plastic sleeve with a metal clip. Drake Kelton, Anesthesiology, was the name on the badge, but the photo was Gabriel Connor. Zane peered closely at it and could see the thin seam where Gabriel had inserted his photo over Dr. Kelton's.

He sent the beam of the penlight back and forth across the space but didn't see any other item in there but the doctor's coat.

He ran his hands along the fabric, feeling for lumps in the jacket pockets or hem. The left pocket had two such lumps and he reached in to grab the items. The first one was a syringe.

The second was a small glass vial with a red top labeled "succinylcholine chloride."

"It's the murder weapon," Zane said out loud.

Now he had to decide what to do. Should he put it back and hope the police found it on their second round through? He didn't want to take the chance. He'd found direct evidence that Gabriel was involved in his girlfriend's death. He had to turn it in. It was time to vacate the premises.

Back in his car, Zane's first text went to Loris, followed by one to Old Spice as Loris instructed.

I've got some evidence you're going to want to see. I think Gabriel Connor killed Dawn Renee.

The response came fast.

Yes, come to the station and fill me in.

When Zane arrived at the headquarters of the Tulsa Police at Civic Center and Sixth in downtown Tulsa, he was already thinking about his exit. He wanted to get the items to Old Spice as soon as possible, but he also knew that the detective was going to have a lot of questions and Zane's day would be shot. Old Spice wasn't going to like the answers.

"Where's your partner?" The greeting, if you could call it that, was a sign that Old Spice was grumpy, and Zane felt sunk. He was going to be sitting in the Detective Division all day.

"She's at the office." Zane held out the plastic bag holding the white coat, the succinylcholine, and the syringe. "You want these or what?"

"What is it?"

Zane told him. Old Spice stood up from his chair and glared down at him. His jaw was rigid, and his eyes so hot Zane thought they might burn a hole through the plastic bag.

"You found this at Gabriel Connor's apartment? And how did you get in?"

Zane fell into full disclosure mode. After all, resistance at this point was futile. He told the detective about Kayla's hunt for her family, about the crypto-currency wallet, about Rittenhour hiring them to clear Tyler Swinton of the charge.

"And you found this where exactly?"

"A false back in the bathroom vanity cabinet," Zane said.

"We missed it," Old Spice admitted.

"Did I just hear you say I helped you?"

Old Spice shrugged, unwilling to concede the point. "So, Gabriel killed Dawn. Why?"

"I don't know. Maybe he was jealous of her, or possessive? I understand they had broken up. But surely you can get at that with a little legwork."

"The prosecutor's not going to like the chain of evidence here. You better not have blown this," Old Spice said but it was a threat without steam or force. He knew as well as Zane did that they had helped break the case and keep an innocent man out of trouble.

It took the Tulsa Police only a few days to find more evidence linking Gabriel Connor to Dawn Renee's death. Video footage had him on camera taking the succinylcholine from the St. Francis pharmacy, and security records showed Drake Kelton's stolen badge being swiped right before. It turned out that the text messages between Gabriel and Dawn on their phones were nothing compared to what was found on their Telegram chat, where they made the most of that service's stellar privacy protections to discuss their "side hustle" business as well as Gabriel's severe jealousy over Tyler Swinton's visits. It seemed Dawn Renee loved secrets. Despite working closely with her boyfriend to hack into companies and hold their data for ransom, she never told him Tyler was her brother. As best as the investigators could tell, Gabriel had killed her in a fit of jealousy after seeing Tyler Swinton leave the house several nights in a row, all without explanation from Dawn.

His jealousy led to his own death. Apparently, Dawn had been the brains behind the data ransom hacking, and when Gabriel couldn't deliver on the latest job, it appeared their criminal partners had taken him out too.

It all seemed simple enough when Old Spice explained it to Loris and Zane.

"What's going to happen to Tyler Swinton?"

"He's already out and there are no charges against him," Old Spice said. "So, your client should be happy."

"Which one?" Loris asked.

"Either," Old Spice said.

Chapter 24
Lettie

Zane knocked on Lettie's bedroom door, and as soon as she could say "come in," Zane was in the doorframe and Ballpoint had leapt onto the bed. Her brother and the dog were excited but for different reasons. Ballpoint's frenzy had to do with the uneaten piece of bread on her plate. Zane's was about Emmaline's sketchy boyfriend.

"Now that we've nearly wrapped up that other case, I ran a background check on Guy Callahan and came up with a hit. This dude has a string of wants and warrants as long as your arm. Priors going back five years."

"What for?"

"Fraud, obtaining property by false pretenses, larceny. Forgery. Bad checks. He's got two warrants on him right now, one in California and the other in Joplin, Missouri. I printed it out."

Zane held out a few sheets of paper stapled together and Lettie took it. She thought she would feel excited at proving her suspicions right, but she mainly felt sad. This was going to cause Emmaline a lot of pain and she didn't want to be responsible for that. She flipped the pages slowly. "Can I keep this?"

"I think we need to give it to Emmaline."

"I get that. But she really likes him, maybe even loves him. I can tell." Doubt and anxiety brimmed up inside her as she stared at the papers. "What if he isn't scamming her? What if he has real feelings for her?"

"Lettie, you don't think that's true."

She gave him a weak smile. "I know. It's just that this feels so hard to do."

"If he's still in town, Detective Pastor said they would pick him up as soon as he had the warrant in hand and the fraud detective in Joplin said he'd make the two-hour drive to get him. Listen, I had to tell the police about his whereabouts, and we have to tell Emmaline about his background. He's been conning people for five years and that's probably just the start. He isn't interested in Emmaline—he's just going to cheat her. What difference does it make how he got caught or who turned him in? Better to do it now before he gets his hands on what little bit of money Em has been able to earn."

"Maybe we tell Emmaline after he's been arrested," Lettie said, hoping to delay the inevitable.

A knock on the front door, followed by the sounds of Verda and Emmaline chatting as they walked toward Lettie's bedroom.

"Zane, Lettie," Verda called out. "It's Emmaline. She needs to take one last length measurement of baby Milly for the dress."

The bejeweled bag that held Emmaline's sewing kit glittered under the fairy lights Lettie had hung around the door frame of her room. "I'm going to have time to finish it up now that Guy is headed back to California for a bit," Emmaline said.

This caught Lettie and Zane by surprise. "He's leaving?"

"Not for good or anything. He's going to San Francisco for

a few days, but he hopes to be back by the end of the week. I guess a little problem came up with one of his partnerships and he has to go fix it. In-person is the only way, he said."

"Is he gone now?"

Emmaline checked her phone. "I don't think so. His plane takes off in five hours or so. He said he had to run a few errands around here and then pack up. Did you want to talk to him?"

Lettie shook her head and folded the piece of paper with the warrant information on it, unwilling to say what she knew she should. Zane stayed silent too.

Emmaline stood in front of them for a long moment, looking at them like they lost their minds. She held a cloth tape measure in her hand and a small pad of paper. "You two are acting weird. Where's Milly?"

She seemed so innocent and happy, nothing more on her mind than finishing that dress. How could Guy take advantage of her?

"Something's come up and we need to tell you something," Zane said. He took the papers from Lettie's grasp and handed them to Emmaline.

"What's this?" She scanned the pages.

Guy's name must have caught her eye because her eyes focused intently on the first page. The smile vanished from her face and her shoulders slumped as she took in the information. When she finished reading, she dropped her hand holding the paper to her side. She was silent for a moment and then looked from Zane to Lettie and back to Zane. "So, I'm the idiot again."

Lettie leaned in to hug her. "Don't say that, Em. I don't think you're dumb. He's a trickster. He's good at fooling people."

"You took a chance on him and he brought you some happiness," Zane said. "Just turns out he's not who he says he is. That's not your fault."

She brought the paper back up to viewing height and looked at it again. "What made you check on him?"

Lettie didn't know what to say, but her big brother stepped in. "Bad vibes, honestly. Me and Lettie both got a bad feeling about him. Call us protective, especially when you started talking about letting him be your manager just when you're starting to make some coin. Have you given him any money?"

Emmaline folded the paper and crossed her arms over her chest. "I went to the bank with him this morning to take out three thousand dollars in cash. He needed it for travel expenses and was going to pay me back. I should have been suspicious when he wanted cash instead of Venmo." Her manner had become very formal, and it nearly broke Lettie's heart.

"I'm going over to Mrs. Ahern's to see if I can catch him before he takes off," Zane said. "Do you want to come?"

Lettie nodded while Emmaline shook her head, her eyes filled with tears. Lettie felt anger in every step they took out of the mobile home and over to Mrs. Ahern's. A white Toyota Prius with ride-sharing stickers peeling off the back window was cruising at half speed, the driver ping-ponging his attention between the mobile phone mounted on the dash and the address numbers on the mobile homes. They all reached Mrs. Ahern's at the same time. The driver pulled over to the curb and Zane ran right up to the driver's side window.

"Are you the one who wanted a ride?" The man squinted at Zane.

"Uh, yes, that's me. Guy Callahan."

The driver didn't even make a show of checking his screen. "Okay, where to?"

"Actually, I don't need the ride anymore. I tried to cancel it on the app but it didn't take."

The driver looked skeptical. Zane reached into his wallet,

found a five-dollar bill, and handed it to him. "For your trouble."

The guy gave him a look, rolled his eyes, and turned to swipe at the screen. He pulled away from the curb and drove off, shaking his head. It was quite the performance of exasperation.

Zane and Lettie crossed to the entrance to Mrs. Ahern's. The older woman was holding the door open, looking anxiously at the departing car.

"I was looking for the Lyft driver," Mrs. Ahern said. "Guy is getting ready to go to the airport. What did you say to him?"

"That guy had the wrong address. He was looking for someone else."

Mrs. Ahern looked skeptical. "Are you here to cause trouble?"

"Not at all," Zane said. Lettie followed him through the living room and into the hall. The door to Guy's room was open.

The space was as bare of Guy's possessions as a hotel room. The drawer where he had hidden the phony IDs was sitting on the floor. A suitcase was packed and sat near the door. A duffle bag was open on the bed, half-filled, and beside it was Guy's phone, charger, and a laptop.

Guy had his back to them, bending over to remove a laptop charger from the wall socket. His jeans were too loose and low, and they could see the bright white skin of his ass. He caught sight of them as he turned. "Oh! You startled me. I thought you were Mrs. Ahern. What's up?"

"We heard you were leaving. Can we help?"

Calculation and uncertainty flickered in his eyes. His quick leave-taking may have been prompted by Lettie's call to his grandparents. Guy might suspect it was her, but he couldn't know for sure. It's not like they were going to confront him.

They were only there to stall him until the police showed up. She wouldn't know how to deal with him, and she didn't think Zane was going to either. They didn't know what he was capable of. Maybe he had a gun or martial arts skills, ready to whip a roundhouse kick at them like a ninja.

"I've got a Lyft coming to give me a ride. I need to stop by the bank on my way to the airport." Guy checked his phone. "That's weird. The ride got canceled."

"We can help," Lettie said. "Zane, you can give him a ride, can't you?"

"Sure, my car's just around the corner. Anyway, you were going to stop by to say goodbye to Emmaline, weren't you?"

"Only if there was time," Guy said. He finished wrapping the charger cord and slipped it into the duffle bag along with the laptop and phone charger. His eyes scanned the room for forgotten items.

"Did you leave anything in the bathroom or kitchen? Laundry?"

"Good thought, yes, in the dryer, I'll be right back." He moved past Zane and Lettie for the laundry room beyond the kitchen.

After Guy left the room, Zane waited a few beats and then reached over to rifle through the duffle bag on the bed. Inside was a plump white envelope with Emmaline's name written on the front in ballpoint pen. It looked to be about thirty hundred-dollar bills. Lettie's eyes widened as she watched Zane close the duffle bag, fold the envelope, and shove it into his coat pocket. He was just adjusting the envelope edges so they didn't poke out of the pocket when Guy returned, toting socks and those bright bikini underwear. He tucked them into the duffle bag and zipped it shut.

"Here, I'll help you," Zane said. He grabbed the duffle bag and Lettie went for the roller bag on the floor, moving into the hallway like Guy's baggage handlers. Mrs. Ahern stood there, nervously checking her phone as though the Powerball Lottery was going to call.

"I can take one of those," Mrs. Ahern said.

"No worries," Lettie and Zane said in unison.

They headed for the front door, with Mrs. Ahern and Guy trailing behind. Where were the cops? Mrs. Ahern and Guy were small-talking up a storm, saying their goodbyes and you mean so much and good luck and it was clear to Lettie that Guy was never, ever coming back. He was leaving the Majestic Mobile Home and RV Park in the rearview mirror.

As they reached the door, Mrs. Ahern moved ahead so she could hold the door open for them. A black SUV with the Tulsa Police's motto "One Tulsa" emblazoned on the side had just pulled up in front. Lettie was afraid if Guy spotted them too soon, he would slip out the back.

"Did you get your phone? Or was it on the bed?" Lettie asked over her shoulder. She paused in the doorway, blocking Guy's view.

Guy patted his pockets. "No, it's right here."

"And the charger?"

"I think so," he said. "Well, maybe I should check." He hurried back to the bedroom while Lettie put the duffle bag on the steps.

Mrs. Ahern stared out the front door in confusion. Two uniformed officers were coming up the path, one male, one female, in their crisp, dark blue pants and short-sleeved shirts. They were not smiling, lending an ominous air. Mrs. Ahern probably thought she had violated some civil code—renting out the room without having a business license or forgetting to pay a parking ticket.

"Guy, your ride is here," Zane said.

"Oh, awesome," he said as he came back into the living

room. "I did find one of the chargers right on the floor so it's good I went back."

As Guy approached the front door, Zane stepped in behind him and Lettie followed suit. Guy glanced up and caught sight of the officers.

The male officer had a nametag that said H. Mummolo. He was white, a little older than Zane, with big arms and a barrel chest. His partner, T. Parks, was thin and wiry.

Mummolo's eyes settled on Guy. "Are you Guy Callahan?"

"Yes?" Guy made it sound like a question, projecting innocence and bafflement. His shoulders stiffened and Lettie thought she could smell the fear on him.

"Could you step out here for us?"

"What's going on?" Guy still held the charger in his hand, the long white cord hanging down like a noose against his legs. He walked down the steps with Lettie and Zane on his heels, luggage in hand.

Mummolo told Guy he was under arrest, reciting his rights to him. Guy's face was a mask of fake surprise and wonderment. "I don't know what this is all about. There must be a mix-up."

"Could you turn around and face the home, please?"

Guy did as he was told, and Parks did a pat-down, then snapped on a pair of handcuffs, all under the watchful eyes of a rattan deer decoration. Guy was starting to get belligerent, his breathing noisy and his legs planted wide. "But what have I done? Nothing. You're making a mistake." His anger seemed to trigger a defense mechanism in Mrs. Ahern.

"What is all this, officers?" she said. "This young man is my tenant. He hasn't done anything wrong."

"Please step back, ma'am," Parks said. "We're going to take Mr. Callahan here downtown and he can contact an attorney then." Parks touched Guy's elbow, but he flinched and pulled away.

"You're making a terrible mistake here," he said, his voice growing loud enough to make a few neighbors look out their windows onto the scene. "Let go of me."

The two officers took control, one on either side, moving him toward the police car quickly. He glanced back at Mrs. Ahern as they hustled him to the back seat, his face a mixture of confusion and pleading. "Don't worry! I'll be all right," he called out. "They'll clear this up and then I'll sue the Tulsa Police for a million dollars for false arrest." Shaking her head, Officer Parks gathered up his luggage and tucked them into the trunk of the SUV.

Mrs. Ahern was red-faced and furious, and she turned to Zane and Lettie. "You two did this. What did Guy ever do to you?"

But Lettie had caught sight of Emmaline about a hundred yards away. Even at that distance, her face seemed blank with disbelief, her body tense. "I'll talk to you later, Mrs. Ahern," Lettie said and headed toward her. Zane followed behind and when they got within ten feet of her, he held out the envelope. Emmaline took it and glanced at the contents. She gave them a searching look, but Zane didn't explain and so Lettie kept quiet too.

"Thank you," Emmaline said.

Back home, Lettie's bedroom was unfamiliar and chilly without Angel. She lay on the bed and tried to imagine what he was doing in Oklahoma City as if they had a mind meld connection. She knew she could just go on Twitch and find out exactly what he was doing in a livestream, but she preferred it this way. She didn't want to see him smiling or happy, or worse, depressed and trying to act happy. The idea of him seeing her in the livestream—seeing her as a betrayer, the one who would not support him—terrified her. They had been through so much together only to have this epic fight erect a nasty wall between them. She couldn't believe he left. She couldn't believe he didn't come back.

Lettie sat frozen on the edge of the bed, staring through the open door as Zane appeared in the doorframe, holding a cooing and happy Milly.

"Do you want me to take her?" Lettie felt deflated and exhausted, and her mood must have come through in her tone because Zane came to sit beside her.

"No, let her have some Uncle Zane time," he said. "She smells so good."

"They say smelling babies releases dopamine, that feel-good neurotransmitter that fuels the brain's reward center. Like meth or cocaine."

"I'll get high from this baby anytime. Hey, Lettie, we did a good thing for Emmaline. She'll see it in time."

"Funny, that's the same line that Angel tells me about this move to Oklahoma City. Maybe I understand more how Emmaline feels than you do. Maybe we want to not have decisions made for us."

"Sometimes we can't see clearly when we look at things solely from our perspective. Other people can have a clearer view."

"You should tell Angel that."

"I would. I did. And I'm telling you too."

Lettie's shoulders sagged. "He doesn't see how this is going to change everything."

"Some changes are good. And I agree with Angel. I don't see how he turns this opportunity down. It could lead to amazing things. And you're acting like you can just toss your feelings for him away like trash."

"If he loved me—"

"Love isn't about control, Lettie. Can you get past that and move into this new chapter with him?"

"Aren't you worried it's going to affect my schoolwork or something?"

Zane shook his head. "If there's one thing I'm not worried about, it's that. And me and Verda, we've decided that we're going to figure out how one of us can go there with you. To help you out."

"It sounds like you're making my decisions for me," she said.

"I am your guardian, at least until you turn eighteen. And I think it's in your best interest to show up for Angel just as he has shown up for you."

"I'll think about it," Lettie said.

Chapter 25
Zane

Zane waved at the video doorbell that Tiffany had installed outside her apartment door, and after a few beats the door swung open. Kayla stood there with a coffee mug in hand.

The women had redecorated a bit. The painting of the woman's face and shoulders with a tree in the background that had hung over Kayla's bed now occupied a spot on the wall behind the dining table. The delicate tree branches and woman's hair curled and spread across a patchy robins-egg blue sky. The thick and glossy paint on translucent vellum paper tempted Zane to trace his fingers over the brush strokes.

"Hello there, Zane," she said.

"This was your mother's painting," he said.

She nodded and shrugged. "Tiffany said she liked the woman's expression and the butterflies and suggested we hang it on this wall. It looks nice out here, doesn't it?"

The image was ethereal in its depiction of nature, yet something seemed out of place the longer he stared at it. His eyes flicked over the elements: the woman and her hair, the tree, the four butterflies, the tangle of shrubs around a tiny pond. A golden key on the banks.

When Zane was a kid, his mom bought him one of those magic eye pictures that change when you stare at them. It was a poster that looked like computerized abstract art, but she told him if he kept staring at it, he would see a recognizable 3D image. He'd lie on the trailer floor staring at that poster for long stretches of time, then get up and stand close to it, trying all the different angles. Nothing worked for a long time. Then one day, his eyes must have gotten so tired that the focus shifted just beyond the image, and *wham!* The image appeared. It was a smiling teddy bear hidden among the repetitive patterns. He could still remember the rush of joy when he conjured the concealed picture. Little did he know that at the age of six, he had already been learning some skills that would come in handy as a private detective.

A golden key on its banks. What he needed to do was shift his focus. Where would Dawn Renee have kept that crypto wallet password so her daughter could find it? It had to be somewhere both obvious and not obvious.

"Do you have a magnifying glass?"

"No," Kayla said, surprised and coming close enough that he could see black liquid sloshing in her coffee mug. "Maybe try your phone camera with the zoom?"

Zane stepped up to the canvas and peered at the golden key, then stepped back to flick on the overhead light and tried again. The shadow of his own head obscured the painting. He moved to see the painted key closer yet couldn't get out of the way of his own shadow. Frustrated, he grabbed his phone from his pocket, turned on the flashlight and the camera, and peered at it through the phone camera's lens.

He yelped and drummed his left hand on his thigh. Four small numbers had been written in impossibly small strokes along the key shaft on this painting. An eight, a three, a one, and six. He shook his head in amazement. It was a fluke. It had been right under their noses all along.

"Kayla, come see this," he said. "Was your mother a painter?"

"Not that I know of." Kayla peered into the phone screen then moved her attention to the painting itself, squinting her eyes to sharpen her vision. "Are those—numbers?"

"Four numbers, to be exact," Zane said. "Isn't that PIN four digits too?"

They stared at the numbers in silence, united in surprise and excitement.

"It's been right in front of me this whole time!" Kayla said, bouncing up and down on her tiptoes.

"Y'all turning into art enthusiasts?" Tiffany's country twang came from behind them, and Zane turned to slip his arm around her as she approached the canvas. Zane pointed his phone light at the spot with the key and showed her the numbers.

"Holy shit," she said. "Is that the PIN?"

The ensuing hours flew by in a mad, nervous headlong rush toward the solution they had all hoped for. It was the PIN. Dawn Renee had left the numbers right where her daughter would find them. All they had to do was shift their focus.

"I'll sell some of it right away to pay you all for your time," Kayla said. "I owe you about what—six thousand dollars?"

"You don't owe us anything," Zane said. "We got a check from Sherwood Rittenhour to cover the expenses." It was news he had been waiting to give her, not sure how she would take it. She stared at his face like he was a book to be read.

"I don't know if I want any of them in my life," she said.

Zane certainly understood that. He'd be just fine if he never saw Sherwood Rittenhour again too.

"It's your choice," he said. "But let him pay for this. He owes you that much." He hoped his conviction resonated in his voice. He felt a swell of sympathy for Kayla, who had gone on a journey to find her family, just like he had, but the happy ending never materialized.

"It's funny but lately I've felt like my mother is with me, an invisible presence. Maybe even an avenging angel, one who made sure Gabriel Connor saw justice."

"Sometimes I feel like my mom is with me too," Zane said. "It makes the world all right for me, even better. Do you think you're going to try to find out who your father is, Kayla?"

"Already looking for another mystery to solve, Zane?" Tiffany batted at his arm.

"No, I just honestly wanted to ask."

"Those are deep waters for me. I have to think about what it would mean if I found him. Like you said at the beginning, sometimes people keep secrets for very good reasons. Right now, I want to focus on what I have in my life, not what's missing. I can do almost anything with one million dollars."

Zane and Tiffany left Kayla to dream about what to do with one million dollars and went to Tally's Good Food Cafe, a 50s diner located on old Route 66 that was open late. They slid into a booth, sitting side by side, Tiffany beaming at him with pride.

"You solved your first case," she said, raising her water glass in a toast.

He raised his glass and clinked it to hers. "I solved my first case," he repeated back, entranced by her smile.

Zane's cell phone dinged with a text notification. He picked it up and saw Lettie's name and the text: *We made it to OKC okay.*

On a whim, Zane launched the Twitch app and looked for Angel's live stream. Sure enough, there he was, online, his broad face filling the screen. His eyes looked watery, but his smile was genuine, wide. The camera angle swung, and Zane saw his sister's face and his grandmother's. Saw Lettie give Angel the tightest of hugs while Verda looked on, holding Milly.

"Did I tell you they have bingo just down the street? Every Tuesday," Angel said.

One word repeated itself in Zane's head. *Family. Family. Family.* Zane felt like a miracle had been worked. He solved his first case. He was surrounded by love.

Acknowledgments

Thank you so much for making it all the way to end. I hope you have enjoyed Zane's fourth story and his new career as a private investigator. If you did, leaving a review is the best possible present for an author!

My most sincere thanks to:

Editor Natalie Cammaratta for her insightful and witty developmental edits to the manuscript. Go buy her book *Falling and Uprising* immediately. She knows how to tell a great story.

Editor and proofreader Cindy Price for her eagle-eyed perspective on missing commas, unclear sentences, and all those little inconsistencies us writers leave in our manuscripts.

To my dear Kaylas, thank you for your support and making me smile. I hope you like Kayla Renee.